Whisper Lake, Another Very Splendor Christmas

Redemption Mountain, Book Twenty-Two
Historical Western Romance

SHIRLEEN DAVIES

Books Series by Shirleen Davies

Historical Western Romances

Redemption Mountain
MacLarens of Fire Mountain Historical
MacLarens of Boundary Mountain

Contemporary Western Romance

Cowboys of Whistle Rock Ranch
MacLarens of Fire Mountain Contemporary
Macklins of Whiskey Bend

Romantic Suspense

Eternal Brethren Military Romantic Suspense
Peregrine Bay Romantic Suspense

The best way to stay in touch is to subscribe to my newsletter. Visit my Website ***www.shirleendavies.com*** and fill in your email and name in the Join My Newsletter boxes. That's it!

Whisper Lake, Another Very Splendor Christmas, is a work of fiction. Names, characters, places, and incidents are either products of the author's imagination or used fictitiously. Any resemblance to actual events, locales, or persons, living or dead, is wholly coincidental.

Book design and conversions by Joseph Murray at 3rdplanetpublishing.com

Cover design by Sweet 'n Spicy Designs

ISBN: 978-1-947680-94-4

I care about quality, so if you find something in error, please contact me via email at

shirleen@shirleendavies.com

Description

He returned a changed man, with a son she knew nothing about.
Will his new life mean the end to what they'd once shared?

Cole Santori faces each day with three goals: be a good father to his adopted son, excel at his job as a Splendor deputy, and do everything possible to convince one woman to give him another chance. He worries little about the first two. The third seems to slip further away with each passing day.

Martha van Plew pursues her passion of helping orphaned children while shoving thoughts of the man she loves aside. Each day is a constant reminder of how he spurned her after returning to Splendor with a son he'd never mentioned.

When a terrible threat faces the children Cole is sworn to protect, they must put their personal issues aside and work together.

The danger escalates until the entire town is on alert for enemies that threaten not just the orphaned children, but also boys and girls living in Splendor. To protect the children, Martha and Cole must use all their resources to eliminate the terror sweeping through the orphanage and their quiet frontier town.

Will their shared danger push Martha to set aside past hurt and open her heart to the man she still loves? Or will a threat as potent as the men hiding in the dark ruin her chance to grasp the future she longs to embrace?

Whisper Lake, book twenty-two in the Redemption Mountain historical western romance series, is a full-length, clean and wholesome novel with an HEA and no cliffhanger.

Whisper Lake, Another Very Splendor Christmas

Chapter One

Splendor Montana
Early December 1873

"Dante!"

Cole Santori's throat constricted, the panic creeping upward from his stomach to his chest. There'd been few times in his life when he couldn't control his emotions. Times such as today. Becoming a father had changed him.

"Dante! Answer me!" His hot breath hit the cold winter air, reminding him of the urgency of the task.

Trudging through the snow, he felt a slight tingling in his toes, as well as a swell of exhaustion. Why had he even considered his son's request to find the caves Cole had told him about? He knew why. The boy's pleading eyes and hopeful expression had gotten to him, weakened his resolve to stay inside until the storm passed.

It had moved on, just not soon enough to provide visibility when Dante ran out of sight.

"Dante! Come out from where you're hiding. It's time to ride back home."

Instead of his son's voice responding, a deep, raspy cough sounded in the still air before shouted words tore through his brain. "Come and get him, Santori."

Cole stilled. He knew the voice, remembered the cough which never went away. The memory speared through him. How had Pierre Hammerstein found him? Cole had been to his trial, heard the jury pronounce him guilty.

"Santori? Can you hear me?"

"I hear you, Hammer." Cole remembered how the man hated the nickname. "What do you want?"

"My name's Pierre."

Cole backed away from the voice to slide behind a boulder. "Do you have my son?"

"I've gotta boy here. Didn't know he was your son, Santori."

That's because they hadn't seen each other in years. Since Cole sent Hammer to prison.

"What are you doing out of prison?"

A brittle laugh set Cole on edge. "Wasn't so hard to break out. It took me a bit to figure what to do. When I did, I found myself on the outside. Isn't that a kick, Santori? And here I am with your son."

"Let him go. The boy has nothing to do with you and me."

Several beats passed before the fugitive spoke. "Maybe not. Still, I'm going to hold onto him for a spell. Ain't that right, son?"

A split second later, Hammer howled in pain. It was followed by the sound of a hand striking flesh. Cole's left hand fisted at his side as his right hand rose, the gun pointing where he was sure Hammer held Dante.

Creeping around the far side of the boulder, Cole moved closer to where Hammer held his son. The ground in this area was covered with the crusty remains of a previous storm. He had to be careful not to let his boots crunch through the layers of ice.

"You still out there, Santori?"

Cole didn't answer as he continued to move behind Hammer. He stilled for a moment when the man holding his son shouted a loud curse.

"I kicked him, Papa!" Dante shouted.

Pride swelled in Cole's chest, along with a good deal of worry. Would the man retaliate? Still, he didn't respond to Hammer's question.

"Your boy is a feisty one, Santori. A lot like his father."

Cole knew he was being baited in an attempt to gauge his position. Edging closer, he could get occasional whiffs of the man's odious scent. He guessed Hammer hadn't been inside a bathtub in weeks. Maybe months.

"Are you still out there, Santori?"

Dante's cry almost had Cole stepping into the open. Instead of giving away his position, he moved closer, careful not to make a sound. Surprise would be the only way to take down Hammer without putting Dante into more danger.

A copse of tall pines clustered at the far side of the boulder. It was what he'd hoped to find.

Sliding behind the thick tree trunks, his breath caught as his anger peaked. Hammer held Dante by the collar of his jacket. The boy's hat was nowhere in sight, the same as the gloves he'd been wearing. Cole tried not to focus on Dante's blue lips or wide, fearful eyes as he aimed his six-shooter at Hammer.

Finger on the trigger, he focused on the man's chest. The shot rang out at the same time Dante slammed his boot a second time on Hammer's foot. The action caused the outlaw to twist, but not in time to avoid the bullet.

A howl escaped as he dropped his hold on Dante to grip his injured shoulder. Realizing the outlaw no longer held him captive, he ran. But not toward his father.

"Dante!" Ignoring Hammer, he retraced his steps to intercept his son before he disappeared into the thickening storm. "Dante, wait!"

Stopping his frenzied escape, Dante's head whipped one way, then another, until he spotted Cole. "Papa!"

Reaching his son, Cole grabbed his arm, rushing both of them toward their horses. A shot hit the ground near them at the same time Cole lifted Dante onto his saddle. Jumping up behind him, he grabbed the reins to his son's horse before rushing them out of range from Hammer's bullets.

Dante warmed his chilled body by the stove in the town's jail while Cole and Sheriff Gabe Evans rifled through two stacks of wanted posters. A deputy in Splendor, he worked days while his son attended school with other children at the new home for orphans.

"This is him." Cole stabbed Hammer's image with his finger. "I thought he was still in prison."

Gabe nodded. "You arrested him?"

"And was the main witness against him. It was my testimony that secured the conviction. It all happened before I came to Splendor."

"How did he find you?"

"I don't know." Cole picked up the wanted poster, studying it more closely. "Hammer had already been taken to Deer Lodge prison when I left Wyoming."

"Here in Montana? Why not a prison in Wyoming?"

"The territorial penitentiary wasn't completed when Hammer was tried." Cole shrugged. "The judge made arrangements to transport him to Deer Lodge."

Gabe sat back, tapping fingers on his desk. "All right. I'll send a telegram to the warden. He'll know if Hammer escaped or was released." He glanced over at Dante, who'd stopped shivering. "His color's returned."

Cole's jaw tightened. "I should've never ridden out with the storm approaching."

"You weren't far from town and couldn't have known the storm would move so quickly."

"I've lived here long enough to understand how fast things change." Scrubbing a hand over his face, Cole shook his head before a small smile tipped the corners of his mouth. "He did great out there. Slammed his boot on Hammer's foot. Twice."

Gabe chuckled, taking another look at Dante. "He's a real warrior."

Cole nodded. "Yeah. I believe he is."

"On Thanksgiving, you mentioned Dante having a rough time at school. Lena asked me if you'd spoken with the administrator, Martha van Plew."

Cole thought of Martha, the woman he'd held an interest in before learning he'd be adopting Danta after his mother's death. Upon their return to Splendor, Martha hadn't pressed him for information about Dante, and he hadn't attempted to provide details. Cole hoped to rectify the standoff soon.

"I haven't spoken to Miss van Plew about it. I'm certain Dante will be all right. It's what you'd expect. There's a boy giving him a hard time, but it will pass." At least, he hoped it would.

Dante and Cole had spent Thanksgiving dinner with Gabe, his wife, Lena, their two children, and Gabe's father, Walter, who'd recently returned from a short trip to New York. Nick Barnett, his wife, Suzanne, and their son, Newt, had also been there, as well as three other deputies.

"You know the two of you are welcome to have Christmas dinner with us."

"Thanks, Gabe. I may take you up on the invitation. Even with the age difference, Dante enjoyed getting to know Jackson." He mentioned Lena's son, who Gabe had adopted soon after their marriage. At thirteen, he was five years older than Dante. Still, they got along well.

"Jack told us Dante seemed older than eight. Said his numbers and reading are better than most of the older children."

"That's all because his mother and her parents sent him to one of the best private schools in Baltimore. He also had a tutor. I believe his advanced abilities are one reason he's being picked on. It's also why he's comfortable around Jack."

"Then you should join us for Christmas dinner. Getting back to Hammerstein, I'll send Wheeler, Taylor, and Nolan to the spot where the outlaw grabbed Dante."

"I'll go with them."

"That won't be needed, Cole. The location you gave me is very clear. It's your day off. You stay with your son and let the boys hunt down Hammer."

The jail's door flew open, cold air rushing in as three of his deputies stepped inside. Morgan Wheeler, Jonas Taylor, and Tucker Nolan brushed snow from their clothes while stomping their boots on the scuffed wood floor.

"Cash told us you wanted to see us," Morgan said, mentioning Cash Coulter, another deputy. His gaze traveled from Gabe to Cole, then Dante.

"I want the three of you to hunt the man in this wanted poster." Gabe held it out to Morgan, who studied it before passing it to Jonas, who handed it to Tucker after reading it.

Gabe explained about Hammerstein grabbing Dante, and Cole rescuing his son. "Cole wounded him."

"In the shoulder," Cole added.

Morgan nodded toward Dante, who stared at the three deputies. "How's he doing?"

Cole smiled at his son. "Doing good, considering what happened."

Gabe pulled a rough drawing of Splendor and the area surrounding the town. "This is where Hammerstein captured Dante."

"He held his gun on me while dragging Dante away." Cole continued to watch his son.

Dante grinned. "I stomped on his foot."

"You did?" Morgan grinned back at him.

"Twice. Then Papa shot him and we got away."

"Well done." Morgan looked at Cole. "How long ago?"

"Over an hour. He couldn't have gotten far."

Before Morgan could ask his next question, the door flew open for a second time. Martha van Plew rushed inside, coming to an abrupt stop at seeing the group of men. She relaxed a little at spotting Dante, though the stress on her features intensified. Her wild gaze landed on Cole for several seconds before moving to the sheriff.

"I need your help right away, Gabe."

Standing, he moved around the desk. "What's happened?"

"One of the children is missing."

Chapter Two

Cole jumped from his chair, going to Martha. Taking her arm, he guided her to the now vacated seat. "Sit down and tell us everything you know."

"I'll get her some coffee." Gabe moved toward the stove, stopping when Martha waved him off.

"No coffee for me, Sheriff."

"Whiskey?"

"I'm fine, Gabe."

Cole could argue the statement. Fine she definitely wasn't.

Gabe sat back down, leaning toward her. "Tell us all you know."

Martha nodded. Hands clasped in her lap, she glanced at Cole. "The children were playing outside. I was standing on the back porch. Rose Keenan and Amy Newhall were in the yard with the children." She paused to inhale and release a shaky breath. "One of the boys, Bobby, had climbed a tree before anyone could stop him. I shouted at him to get down. Amy was waiting for him at the base of the tree. Almost all the children stopped what they were doing to cluster around the tree and watch. Rose joined Amy. My attention was on Bobby. He'd started to move, but froze, pointing to a spot at the far edge of the yard. Well, what we consider the boundary of how far the children can get from the house."

"Did you see what Bobby was pointing to?" Cole asked.

"No. I took a quick look before my attention focused back on Bobby. An older boy climbed up to help him down. That's when he said a man had tugged another boy through the trees." She wrung the hands in her lap. "It's so awful."

"Did you get a description of the man?"

"I did, Sheriff. Bobby said he wore a long black coat and a black hat. That's all he could tell us."

Gabe flashed a look at Cole, giving a slight shrug. He got the sheriff's meaning. "Martha, did Bobby have any idea how tall the man might be?"

"I'm sorry, Cole, but no. A black coat and hat are all he could tell us."

"Did he mention a horse?"

She shook her head. "No."

Cole looked at Gabe, silently asking the sheriff to take over.

"The boy he took is one of the orphans, right?" Gabe asked.

"Yes. He's twelve. His name is Theodore, but everyone calls him Teddy."

"Morgan, Jonas, and Tucker. Ride out to the orphan home and start a search. I'll find a few other deputies and have them ride back with me and Miss van Plew." He waited until the three left the jail before turning to Cole.

"Could this be the man we were discussing?"

Cole gave a sharp shake of his head. "Hammer was wounded. I doubt he could control Teddy and get him away from the school with one good arm."

"Did he ever ride with a partner?"

"The men he rode with were either dead or scattered when I arrested him. It's been over two years since he went to prison. It's doubtful he's been able to find any men who are still alive since he escaped, or was released."

"Reminds me. I need to send a telegram to the warden. Martha, this won't take long. When I return, we'll ride together to the orphanage."

"Thank you, Sheriff. I appreciate any help you can provide."

Standing, she glanced at Dante before looking at Cole. "This won't come out right, but I'm glad this didn't happen when the children from town were in school. Who knows what the man would have done."

"We won't know what would've happened. I'll ride out with Dante to help with the search."

She shook her head. "No. Stay with your son."

An uncomfortable silence washed over them. Cole wanted to reach out and take her hand, tell her the story of him and Dante. Now wasn't the time. Yet he hadn't been able to find the right time since returning from New York months earlier.

"We need to talk. Would you be available to have supper with me sometime soon?"

Martha swallowed. She'd expected an invitation from Cole soon after his return to Splendor. When weeks passed without him asking, she'd decided he no longer held an interest in her.

"I don't know. I'm awfully busy. Most days, I don't go home in the evening but stay overnight at the orphanage."

He wouldn't allow his disappointment to show. "Will you at least consider supper?"

Both turned when the door opened. Gabe walked inside "Are you ready, Martha?"

"Yes." She glanced at Cole. "Yes, I am, Sheriff." Without answering Cole's question, she rushed outside into the diminishing storm.

"Do you like Miss van Plew, Papa?"

Cole whirled around to face his son, his mouth twisted in confusion. "Of course, I like her. She's your teacher."

"But do you like her *like her*?"

Brows scrunched together, Cole crossed his arms. "I think Miss van Plew is an excellent person. Now, we need to get home."

"What about getting our Christmas tree?"

Cole felt relief he'd been able to steer the subject away from Martha.

"I'm sure I can find it again," Dante added, his voice full of hope.

Dante had picked the perfect tree an instant before Hammer appeared out of nowhere and grabbed him. Cole had no intention of putting his son back into potential danger.

Dante tried once more. "We should go back and get the tree I picked out, Papa."

"I don't think that's a good idea. Not with Mr. Hammerstein roaming around. Get your boots back on. We'll take the horses to Noah's livery, then go home. If it's not snowing in the morning, we'll get a tree."

"Great!" Dante rushed to put on his boots and coat. "I'm ready."

Chuckling, Cole slipped on his coat. "Let's go before the storm picks up again."

Noah Brandt and his wife, Abigail, owned several businesses, and most of the houses in town. Cole and Dante lived in one of them. The livery, where he'd also been the blacksmith, had been his first business.

Cole didn't have a place to keep his horses. It was the same for most people who lived in town. Over time, Noah had increased the size of the livery several times until it now held close to thirty horses.

They left their two geldings in the stalls Noah designated before walking the short distance to the house. It was a nice place with two bedrooms, a kitchen, and a living room big enough for a table where they ate their meals.

"Wash up while I heat the stew."

"Yes, sir."

Watching Dante run off, Cole thought of how much his life had changed since a year earlier. He'd never imagined Dante's mother would die so young, leaving her son's care in the hands of a roving lawman. Cole felt humbled by the trust she put in him. It was an odd coincidence he'd already decided Splendor would be his home. Dante entering his life made it more so.

"Papa. When will we leave tomorrow to get my tree?"

Stoking the cookstove while adding more wood, he returned to stirring the stew. "After breakfast. It would be best to find a different tree."

"Do you think the Hammer man will still be there?"

Cole couldn't stop a chuckle at his son's title for the outlaw. "He might still be close to where I shot him. To be safe, we'll look closer to town."

"Can we take Jackson with us?"

"It would be best for the two of us to go alone, son. There's a stand of beautiful trees behind a building Mr. Brandt uses to store furniture left behind when people move out of Splendor. I'll ask him if he'd mind us chopping down our tree on his land."

Dante's face fell. "I thought we'd bring home my tree."

"It'll still be your tree, son. It just won't be the one you picked out this morning."

"Okay..." Slumping onto the sofa, he stared out the window.

"Don't get comfortable. You need to set the table for supper."

"Grandma used to set the table while Mama made our meals."

Cole knew this, as Dante had mentioned it more than once. "I know, son. Now it's your responsibility. If you'd rather cook, I'll set the table."

Dante laughed at the idea, the exact action Cole hoped would come from his suggestion. "You should cook, Papa." Jumping up, he rushed into the kitchen for what he needed. When finished setting the table, he moved next to Cole. "What did the Hammer man do, Papa?"

"He tried to kidnap you."

Dante's brows drew together. "Not today. When you sent him to prison."

"Oh, right. He killed another man. Mr. Hammerstein killed several people."

"He's a very bad man."

"That he is, son."

"Why did they let him out of prison if he was so bad?"

"We don't know if he was released or escaped. The sheriff is trying to find out. What matters now is he tried to kidnap you."

"Because you arrested him, right?"

Letting out a deep breath, Cole nodded. "That's what I believe."

"Will he come after me again?"

"Not if he's smart. He'll get as far away from Splendor as possible." He already knew Hammerstein couldn't read or write, but that didn't mean he was stupid. It didn't mean he'd make smart choices, either.

"I know Teddy."

Cole blinked a couple times, trying to recall Teddy. "The boy who was taken from the orphanage?"

"Uh-huh. He's quiet and real smart. We sometimes do our numbers together."

"Teddy is twelve."

"I know. He and Jackson are friends."

"The sheriff's son?"

Dante nodded, his eyes dulled with concern. "I hope Teddy is all right."

"We all hope so, son."

A loud knock on the front door had both turning toward it. "I'll get it, Papa."

"No. You stay in the kitchen while I see who it is." Walking to where he'd hung his holstered gun, he drew out the six-shooter. He didn't believe Hammerstein would knock, but Cole wouldn't take any chances.

Holding the gun to his side, he opened the door, blowing out a relieved breath. "Gabe. Come in." Standing aside, he motioned for the sheriff to enter.

"I wanted to let you know what the prison warden said before riding out to the orphanage." Gabe cast a quick glance at Dante before looking back at Cole. "Hammerstein escaped last week."

Chapter Three

Martha sat next to Gabe as he maneuvered the wagon over deep, bumpy ruts and out of town. His horse was tied to the back, reminding her he would be joining his deputies in the search for Teddy. Behind them, three more deputies followed with serious expressions. Cash Coulter, and brothers, Hex and Zeke Boudreaux, would join the three the sheriff had already sent out.

She couldn't help the fear wrapping around her heart. Sending up a quick prayer for Teddy to be returned safe and sound. What Gabe and Cole had discussed at the jail bothered her a great deal.

"Did I understand a convict at Deer Lodge may have escaped and tried to take Dante?"

Gabe didn't respond right away. When he did, his voice was grave. "Yes. Pierre Hammerstein is the man who attempted to ride off with Dante. I learned he had escaped from Deer Lodge."

"The warden confirmed he got away?"

"Yes. If you're thinking he also took Teddy, that would be doubtful. Cole wounded him. If Teddy struggled at all, he would've been able to break loose from whoever took him."

"Maybe there'll be a demand for money when we reach the orphanage."

"Maybe." Gabe's voice didn't hold any conviction in Martha's theory.

"You doubt it?"

"Martha, I have no idea who took Teddy or why. It's sometimes best not to guess."

Her chest heaved on a shaky breath. "I can't stop wondering what's happening to Teddy. If the man has hurt him…" Her voice faltered, making it impossible to continue the thought.

"It would be best for you to focus on the children still at the orphanage. Let me and my deputies look for Teddy."

"I'm certain you're right, Sheriff. Unfortunately, turning off my concern for Teddy is beyond my ability."

Falling silent, Gabe took the last turn before arriving at the orphanage. Martha had been in charge of the renovations. When they were completed, Reverend Paige's wife, Ruth, had asked her to continue on as the administrator until they could find a satisfactory replacement. The house had gone from an eyesore to a showplace.

Amy Newhall stood on the front porch, her features drawn. She hurried down the steps when the wagon came to a stop. Martha stepped to the ground without waiting for Gabe's assistance.

"Any sign of Teddy, Amy?"

Her shoulders slumped. "No. I was hoping you might have news of him."

"Gabe sent three deputies to start the search. Are they here?" Martha asked.

"They spoke to Rose and me before talking to Bobby."

Martha glanced at Gabe. "That's the boy who climbed the tree."

"When the deputies were finished asking questions, they mounted their horses and spread out to start the search. I don't know when they'll be back. Will those deputies search, also?" Amy nodded to the three men who'd ridden to within a few feet of the wagon.

"Yes," Gabe answered. "I'll be searching with them."

"Give me a few minutes to change and I'll go with you." Martha turned to rush to the house, stopping when Gabe's single word response hit her.

"No."

"No?"

"I'd rather you stay here with Rose, Amy, and the children. The three of you should take all the children downstairs."

"To the basement?" Martha protested.

"Your basement is better than most living rooms in Splendor."

She waved him off. "Amy and Rose can take care of the children."

Gabe shook his head, knowing he should've prepared himself for Martha's well-known streak of stubbornness. "Are you able to shoot both a rifle and six-shooter?"

"Well...no."

"Do you have a horse?"

She shook her head, beginning to understand.

"Stay here, Martha. Let me and my men take care of finding Teddy."

Exhaling a deep breath, she gave a slow nod. "All right."

Walking to the back of the wagon, he untied his horse and swung into the saddle. "Take the children straight to the basement."

"Yes, of course. We'll get them down there right away."

Touching the brim of his hat, Gabe reined his horse around to join the others. Martha watched the four men ride toward the back of the house and disappear. She hated staying behind, but realized there wasn't much she could do to help with the search.

Amy and Rose waited inside, where they'd gathered the children. Martha stopped several feet away to scan the faces of each one. They were eerily quiet, their expressions tense.

"Miss van Plew?"

She hadn't seen the girl leave the group to stand by her side. Six-year-old Alice grabbed the material of Martha's skirt, looking up with wide, sad eyes.

"Yes?"

"Where's Teddy?"

Dropping to kneel beside her, Martha placed both hands on the girl's shoulders. "The sheriff and his men are searching for him. I'm certain it won't be long before they bring him home."

"Oh..." The girl didn't sound convinced. "Bobby said a bad man took him."

"He's right, Alice."

"What if he hurts Teddy? People get hurt all the time. My mama and papa got hurt, and I didn't see them again."

Martha's heart squeezed, a pain which never lessened at hearing how each child had lost their parents. Some became orphans when their mothers and fathers simply rode off and left them. She'd never understand how parents could leave their children behind.

"I know, sweetheart. And now you live here with us."

"All right, children." Amy stood at the top of the stairs to the basement. "Form a line starting here." She pointed to a spot next to her. "When everyone's in line, we'll go down the stairs."

"To the basement?" Jeramy, a boy of eight, flashed her a brilliant smile.

"That's right." Amy focused on the waiting children. "We're going to have a great time."

Alice left Martha to take her place with the others. Rising, she joined Rose. "How are the children doing?"

"All right. Asking about Teddy. It will be better when it's safe for them to go outside. At least the basement is large. You were wise to have the men finish it the same as the upstairs."

"I wish I'd been wise enough to add windows."

"Windows in a basement?"

"I've seen them in many of the larger houses and buildings back east. Unfortunately, this house wasn't built for them." Martha watched the children follow Amy down the steps, each gripping the handrail. It struck her again how none of them spoke. The quiet was unsettling.

Taking her place at the back of the line, she followed them down the stairs. The silence continued to bother her. Never again would she groan at the laughter and constant chattering of the children.

Several hours passed without word from Gabe. The three women played games with the children, reading to the younger children while the older ones selected their own books. Rose organized a play about the townsfolk of Splendor. Each child selected a role while the women acted as their audience.

Amy prepared meals, which two older children helped her carry down the stairs. Martha watched in wonder. What she'd first believed would be a difficult adjustment had turned into an adventure.

All the children were given time to collect bedding to carry downstairs. The large basement accommodated everyone. The boys were on one end of the room and girls on the other. Amy, Rose, and Martha selected spots in the center, spreading out their own blankets.

After the excitement of the play and food eaten from plates on their blankets subsided, the children drifted off to sleep. The women took turns staying awake to watch over them and listen for Gabe's return.

Martha took the middle shift, making certain Rose and Amy each had at least six hours of sleep. Rearranging her blankets and pillow against a wall, she propped herself against it. Wide awake, her thoughts drifted to Cole.

It still puzzled her why he hadn't made any attempt to explain the appearance of Dante. A wonderful boy with a keen mind and subtle sense of humor, he'd settled in with both the orphans and children from town. But where had he been living before arriving in Splendor?

Martha considered Cole's invitation to supper, the first one offered since his return. She could still recall the disappointment which claimed her each time he dropped Dante off for school. He'd made no attempts to talk with her. The same when he arrived to take his son home when school ended.

After training Dante to ride a horse, Cole allowed him to accompany the other town children to and from school. The horse he rode was an older, calm mare. Martha knew this since she'd ridden Beauty herself several times. Safe and dependable is how Noah Brandt described the mare Cole had borrowed for Dante.

Martha tried to recall Cole's history before he arrived in Splendor. She knew he'd been a deputy in Wyoming, but that period wouldn't account for Dante being eight years old. Cole had to have met the boy's mother before then. She wished he'd shared more of his history with her. To find answers, she'd have to accept his invitation to supper.

Closing her eyes, she smiled at the recollection of the last meal they'd shared before his trip back east. He'd taken her to the Eagle's Nest in the St. James Hotel.

It had taken her over an hour to select a dress and fix her hair. The food had been spectacular, even if the mood at the table had been less than cheery.

Before that evening, it had been a while since he'd stopped by to visit. He'd cited his long hours as a deputy, and the fact he often worked nights. She'd been less than impressed with his excuses, passing on his attempts to smooth over the missteps. Knowing he might be gone for a while, she'd finally relented just before he left Splendor.

Now he was back, with a son she'd known nothing about, and no sense of urgency to provide an explanation. Martha knew she should ignore him as he had her. Manners drilled into her by her parents, and practiced at hundreds of social events while growing up, forced her to be the gracious woman her family would expect.

Tugging the blanket up to ward off the chill, Martha made her decision. She'd attend supper with him, if for no other reason than to learn more about Dante, his mother, and Cole's connection to both.

Chapter Four

"That one, Papa!" Dante pointed to a thick pine about eight feet tall and almost as wide.

Cole inspected the tree, wondering how he'd get it home without a wagon. "It sure is a beautiful tree, son."

Dante's smile was quick and wide. "I know. Can we chop it down now?"

"We can, except I don't know how we'll get such a large tree home." Cole not only worried about the size. With the branches heavy with snow, the weight bothered him. He knew Dante would try to help, though his skinny frame wasn't strong enough to do much.

"Maybe Mr. Brandt could help."

"He's a busy man, son."

"What about Sheriff Gabe?"

"He's looking for your friend, Teddy."

"Oh…" Dante walked around the tree, which dwarfed him, his face scrunched in thought.

"What about a smaller tree?"

Crossing his arms, he glared at Cole. "This is the one I want."

"It is beautiful. I'll bet there's another one as nice that would be easier to get home."

The sudden gunshot froze Dante in place.

"Get down!" Cole shouted while drawing his six-shooter from the holster. When his son didn't react, he closed the distance between them, avoiding another bullet as he tackled the boy to the ground. "Stay down until I tell you to move."

"Okay," Dante choked out.

Another bullet hit the ground a foot away. This time, Cole saw the flash from the gun's barrel. Shifting his position above Dante, he fired three shots in the direction where the shooter hid in the low brush and trees. Moments later, they heard a horse's whinny along with pounding hooves on the icy ground.

Cole pushed up to his knees, his worried gaze scanning Dante. "Are you all right?"

Popping up as if nothing had happened, Dante nodded. "Let's go after him."

If he hadn't been so scared for his son, Cole might've laughed. "I want you to stay here. I'll be right back."

Dante's face fell. "I want to come with you."

Cole could see the fear in the boy's eyes. "All right, but you stay right next to me."

"I will."

Chasing whoever shot at them wasn't on his mind. He planned to search the area where the shooter hid like a coward, targeting a man and young boy hunting the perfect Christmas tree. Checking the ground, brush, and rocks, he found nothing to indicate any of his bullets had hit the intruder. Not a drop of blood anywhere.

"We need to get back to town."

"But the tree..."

"We'll come back, Dante. Right now, we need to notify the other deputies about what happened."

"Promise we'll come back?"

Setting a hand on his son's shoulder, Cole nodded. "Promise."

He grabbed Dante's hand and rushed to their horses. They weren't far from the jail. Not more than a few minutes away.

Cole shouldn't have been surprised at how well Dante controlled his horse on the crowded streets. At eight, he'd expected him to be more hesitant riding his mount around wagons and people rushing across Splendor's main street.

Reaching the jail, they slid to the ground, tossed the reins over the hitching posts, and headed inside. Deputy Beth Evans, Gabe's sister-in-law, sat at the desk, reviewing wanted posters. Looking up, she smiled.

"Hello, Dante. How's your father treating you?"

Giggling, the boy walked to stand next to her. "He treats me okay."

"Only okay?" She winked at Cole.

"Maybe more than okay." He glanced at his father before giggling again.

Shaking his head, Cole sat down. "Has Gabe returned?"

"No. He did send Morgan Wheeler back to let us know they hadn't found Teddy. Gabe wanted another group of deputies to ride out to take the place of those who searched overnight."

"Who did he send back out?"

"Everyone left, except for you and me." She pointed to her expanding stomach.

Cole smiled. "How much longer?"

"Doc McCord says about another month. I hope he's right." Sighing, she returned to the wanted posters.

"I'm going to ride out to the orphan home to let Miss van Plew know someone shot at Dante and me while we were out behind Noah's extra building."

Beth had been a federal agent before marrying Gabe's brother and settling in Splendor. Not much shook her. Eyes wide, she shoved herself up before grabbing her gun from the desk.

"Chan is in town." She mentioned her husband, Gabe's youngest brother, Chandler. "The three of us can search for him."

Fighting a grin, he shook his head. "I doubt your husband would allow you to hunt a gunman in your condition."

Blowing out a breath, she set her gun back on the desk. "You're right. A search should be started soon."

"I know." Standing, he looked at Dante. "I'm riding out to the orphan home. You need to stay in town."

"He can stay with me, Cole." Beth moved her gaze to Dante. "Does that suit you?"

Looking at his father, Dante saw the resolve on his face. "Yes."

"That's nice of you, Beth. Thank you." Cole closed the distance between himself and his son. "I know you'll be good for Deputy Evans. What I want you to do is keep watch for anyone who doesn't look right to you."

"Who might want to shoot at us?"

"That's right, son. You study the people outside and let her know if anyone looks suspicious."

Dante's brows drew together. "What's suspicious?"

"Well, now...someone who doesn't look like he belongs."

"Like the man who tried to take me?"

"Exactly like him. You tell Deputy Evans right away."

"I will, Papa."

Beth hid a grin. "He'll be at our house whenever you get back."

"I may not return tonight."

"That's all right. He can stay with us as long as necessary."

Cole thanked her again. Hugging Dante, he hesitated at the door a moment before leaving to hunt down a kidnapper.

Martha paced the large back porch while watching the children play. Worry over the children had impacted her sleep, as well as Rose's and Amy's.

She knew they couldn't keep the children in the basement much longer. If she'd received news from Gabe or one of his deputies about Teddy...but she hadn't. The decision to relent and allow them outside that morning had been difficult. Instead of one of the women watching them, all three kept an uneasy vigil. From her location, Martha had a good view of the area behind the informal play area.

Maybe she should've ordered fences around the property, the same as some wealthy homeowners did back east. But this wasn't Boston or New York, and most of the churchwomen weren't wealthy. Martha and a few of the wealthier townsfolk had contributed to the fund used to clean and repair the house. Their money continued to fill the pantry with food and provide school books and other supplies. Building a fence had never been a consideration.

Resting her hands on the top railing, she began to compose a mental list of changes at the orphanage. The first would be getting an estimate from Noah Brandt on the cost of a fence.

The children's laughter brought her focus back to the play area. Young boys and girls had a wonderful habit of rebounding from bad situations. She was glad for that while knowing there would still be questions about Teddy when the children returned to the schoolroom.

The sight of three riders approaching the orphanage had her straightening. Her gaze darted to the children, then back to the riders.

"Amy! Rose! Please bring the children inside."

The women didn't hesitate. It took little time for the children to rush into the house and to their desks in the schoolroom. Rose stood at the front, explaining what they'd be studying. Amy stood at the back, dividing her attention between the children and watching out the window as the men on horseback rode closer. She expected to see the deputies, but Amy didn't recognize any of them.

Martha appeared in the doorway, motioning Amy to join her in the hall. A shotgun in each hand, she lowered her voice.

"Take this." She handed over one of the shotguns before reaching into the pocket of her dress to retrieve extra shells. "Find a spot near a window in the living room. Don't do anything until we know what the men intend."

Nodding, Amy did as Martha said.

Leaving the second shotgun leaning against a wall, Martha motioned for Rose to join her. Handing her the shotgun, she sent her to the front office.

"I'll get the children downstairs before taking a spot in the living room."

"You'll talk to them first, Martha?"

"I'm not sure what I'm going to do."

"It might be best to wait until we know what the men will do. Maybe you'll recognize them." Rose shrugged before walking toward the office.

Ushering the children down to the basement didn't take long. She could see in the expressions of the older children they knew something wasn't right.

"Don't come upstairs until one of the adults tell you it's safe."

"Yes, Miss van Plew." The chorus of responses warmed her, solidifying her determination to keep them away from harm.

Amy sat in a chair she'd scooted to a window in the living room. "What's happening, Amy?"

"Nothing. They're sitting on their horses."

"Are any of them familiar?"

Amy shook her head. "No. Maybe you'll recognize them."

Martha held the curtain back a few inches. Peering out, she blinked a few times before focusing on the faces of the three men. She moved from one man to the next before settling on the third man.

Her breath caught, certain she was looking at the man who'd taken Teddy.

Chapter Five

Cole rode toward the orphanage, exhaustion coursing through him. He'd encountered Gabe and his fellow deputies when he rode out late the previous day. Tired and disappointed after almost three days and little progress locating Teddy, Gabe had already decided they'd return to Splendor.

Cole had protested until he understood the sheriff's plan to organize a much larger search group. Noah Brandt, Nick Barnett, Dax and Luke Pelletier, and many others would volunteer. Men who knew the area, the location of hidden caves, and less traveled trails. Places where a kidnapper could hide for days.

He'd spent the night in their camp, listening to the men share where they'd already searched. They didn't last long talking around the campfire. All needed a few hours of sleep. Even wearing their clothes and coats to bed, they still shivered in the winter cold.

Gabe broke camp before sunup, anxious to return to town. Forming a large search effort would take time. More time than he wanted to spend, but he and his deputies couldn't continue the way they'd been going.

Cole continued to the orphanage, expecting to find Martha and everyone else safe. The scene he came upon didn't strike him as safe.

Three men sat atop their horses, their gazes fixed on the house. When the front door opened and Martha stepped outside with a shotgun positioned against her shoulder, he knew it was time to make his move.

Shoving his coat aside, he drew his six-shooter. Pushing his heels into his horse's sides, he rode forward at a slow pace, the gun ready to gun down anyone who threatened Martha.

Martha stepped closer to the edge of the porch, the shotgun aimed at the riders. Three men against one woman. A city woman who'd probably never held a shotgun before today. Cole knew she'd be dead, even if she did manage to hit one of them.

Riding closer, he saw the instant Martha noticed him. She didn't flinch or give his presence away by turning toward him. He would've smiled if the situation had been different.

Cole rode to within ten yards of the men, his gun trained on the one whose horse stood a few feet in front of the others. *The leader*, he thought, nudging his horse closer. The man nearest to him glanced over his shoulder. Startled, he went for his gun.

"Don't," Cole warned, his hard voice as menacing as his six-shooter. "What's going on, Martha?"

"They believe we're addlebrained women with a bunch of unruly children in tow. I assured him that wasn't the case."

He wondered what the man's comment meant, and his true intent. "It's time the three of you move along. There's nothing for you here."

The leader reined his horse around to face Cole. "Talking to this fine woman makes me want to stay."

"At an orphanage with a group of unruly children? I'm certain you'll find better entertainment elsewhere."

Another of the men sneered at him. "Who are you to tell us what to do?"

"Deputy Santori." He moved his horse closer, his gun never wavering. "Who are you three?"

The men looked at each other, a silent message seeming to pass between them. Without another word, they reined their horses away from town and rode off.

Cole didn't holster his gun until the men had disappeared on the southbound trail. There was a choice to be made. Stay to protect the women and children if the men returned or follow them to make sure they didn't turn back in this direction. He chose the first.

Sliding into four inches of snow on the ground, he rushed up the steps, ushering Martha inside as the wind whipped around them. Brushing off his coat and striking his hat against his thigh, he faced Martha.

"Do you believe any of those men were involved in taking Teddy?"

She rubbed her hand against her forehead. "I don't know, Cole. No one got a good look at him."

"Not even Bobby, the boy in the tree?"

"I'm afraid not. He hasn't been able to provide a better description than what he already gave us." She pressed fingers to her temples, letting out a weary sigh. "I know those men today were up to something, Cole. I wish I knew what. What do you think?"

"Could be several reasons for why they stopped here. Hunger, sleep, to get out of the cold…"

"Or to steal children." Her voice was flat, void of all emotion.

"Yes."

Tired legs carried her to the living room, where she lowered herself onto an upholstered chair. Cole had seen similar furniture. Lots of it in his parents' New York mansion. He joined her on a nearby chair.

"I believe they were trying to discover if there are men here to protect you and the children."

Martha's face paled, her expression tense. "And I gave away it's just women and the children."

"They probably already knew this."

"They were just confirming their suspicions?"

"Makes sense," Cole confirmed.

Rising, she paced in a small circle, continuing to rub her temples. "I don't understand their intentions."

Cole's brows drew into a frown. "What do you mean?"

"Well, assuming one of them took Teddy, why do they want to check about men at the orphanage? Do they intend to take more children? If so, what do they want with them? Are they after specific children, or whichever ones are easiest to take?" She stepped to a window, peering through the curtains, then whirled around to face Cole. "It seems I'm rambling."

"You're asking legitimate questions." Walking to her, he set his hands on her shoulders, his calming gaze helping her to relax. "And you aren't rambling. There are too many unknowns right now. We aren't even certain they're the ones who took Teddy. All we know is those three men have an interest in the orphanage." Dropping his hands, he stepped away.

"What should I do?"

"That's what we have to decide. One step we must take is to hire a few men to guard everyone until we know what they want, if anything."

Walking around him, Martha crossed her arms. "We have no budget to pay them."

"Do you disagree a few men are needed?"

She shook her head. "Not at all. I just don't know where we'll get the money to pay them."

"Don't worry about payment right now. What's important is to keep everyone safe. Agreed?"

Drawing in a slow breath, she let it out, her back going rigid. "I'll do whatever it takes to keep Amy, Rose, and the children safe."

Gabe left seven deputies in town. The remaining seven joined twenty-three men who'd volunteered to search for Teddy.

He looked over the group of thirty men, seeing determination mixed with anger on their faces. Gabe understood. The two emotions paired well when hunting down a man who'd kidnapped a child. Even more so when the victim had already suffered the loss of his parents, leaving him an orphan.

"Are there any questions as to where we'll be searching?"

When no one spoke, he shot a look at his deputies. "As mentioned earlier, each group is led by one of my men. We don't want to lose any of you to the kidnapper, so stay vigilant. I'll be at the orphanage in case the kidnapper returns. All right. Let's get going."

Gabe waited until the last group rode out of town before mounting his horse to join Beth. They'd ride together to the orphanage.

The instant the two-story, white home came into sight, his gut began to twist. Cole's horse was outside. Even when the children were inside, there always seemed to be someone outside.

They hadn't dismounted when the front door opened, Cole stepping onto the porch. His gaze moved from the sheriff to the area beyond. He saw nothing suspicious in the trees.

Cole let out a relieved breath. "I'm glad you're here."

"What's happened?"

Opening the door, Cole motioned for them to go inside. "Martha had visitors."

Gabe opened his mouth to speak, stopping the response when he spotted Martha. The woman who always held a smile for visitors didn't offer an immediate welcome. Today, her features were grim, face pale, mouth pinched.

"Hello, Sheriff, Deputy Evans. May I offer you any refreshments?"

Both shook their heads as Cole stepped next to her. "You need to tell them what happened. Or would you prefer I explain?"

"If you don't mind. We can sit at the dining room table."

When all were seated, Cole described the encounter with the three men. "They rode off, but I doubt they'll stay away."

Martha glanced at Cole, feeling a pinch around her heart. She was glad he'd shown up when he did, relieved at his decision to stay. It had been a long time since they'd spent time together. Though her duties at the orphanage kept her busy, she missed seeing him. Forcing thoughts of what could've been aside, she concentrated on the discussion Cole was having with Gabe and Beth.

"There isn't an issue with me staying," Gabe said.

Beth leaned forward. "Chan is delivering a prisoner to Deer Lodge prison, so I can stay."

"That would be wonderful," Martha said, feeling her tense body relax. "We need to get the children back outside, but after the three men showed up, I've been hesitant."

Gabe stood. "You made the right decision. Two of us will be with them while they're playing outside. The third deputy will be guarding the front. We'll rotate positions. There's a good chance the search party will locate Teddy. If we're lucky, they'll arrest the kidnapper."

Cole didn't share Gabe's optimism, though he was smart enough to keep quiet.

Martha clasped her hands in her lap. "Should we continue having the children sleep downstairs?"

"For now," Gabe answered. "It will be easier for us to guard them."

They spent several more minutes discussing details before taking positions around the house. Cole hesitated leaving Martha alone. The woman he'd first met appeared to have aged over the last few days. He knew she wasn't taking the danger to the children well, yet she fought to stay strong. His appreciation for her had grown a great deal in the last twenty-four hours.

"I'll be on the front porch, Martha."

"All right." When he turned to leave, she touched his arm. "I'm glad you're here, Cole."

A tight smile lifted the corners of his mouth. "I'm glad, too. Real glad."

A moment later, the two were even more grateful for his presence when a broken cry came from the front of the house.

Chapter Six

Martha beat Cole to the front door, and would've gone outside if Cole hadn't grabbed her arm.

"You stay in here until I know what's out there." Drawing his six-shooter, he opened the door.

"Be careful, Cole."

Glancing over his shoulder, he gave a quick nod before closing the door behind him. Dropping to a crouch, he inched forward while scanning the area. He heard another loud cry, this one deeper than the first. Certain it was human and not an animal, he moved to the edge of the porch.

He listened for several minutes. When he heard nothing more, he began edging back to the front door.

"Help me…"

The croaked plea sounded close. Very close.

Looking around once more, and seeing nothing, he rushed down the steps. He dropped to his knees to peer under the porch. At first, he saw nothing. Then he spotted a shivering form huddled a few feet away. A young boy's face appeared, wide eyes filled with fear.

"Can you crawl to me?"

The boy didn't respond right away. He opened his mouth to respond, then closed it. Cole noticed his lips were colored a deep blue against a pale face. Instead of trying to answer, he scooted forward, wincing with each movement.

Cole holstered his gun before reaching into the darkness with both hands. Small, ice cold hands brushed his. Cole wrapped his hands around the boys arms, tugging him forward. The boy pulled his arms free, attempting to wrap them around Cole's waist. That's when the deputy heard the quiet crying.

He circled the boy in his arms, hugging him close as he rose. Scanning the area and seeing nothing to alarm him, Cole rushed up the steps. That's when he saw Martha standing with the door open. A hand moved to her chest.

"Oh, my lord."

Cole hurried past her to the kitchen, where he knew there'd be a fire in the cookstove. He wasn't disappointed. The boy's crying had stopped by the time he set him on a chair.

"Here, take these." Martha held out a towel, setting dry clothes on the counter. "I'll prepare a warm bath."

The boy looked up at her, dried tears staining his dirty face. Her heart stuttered at the sight. She reached over to touch his cheek, dropping her hand when he flinched.

"Would you want to hold him while I prepare the bath?" Cole asked.

She shook her head. "I don't believe he'd be comfortable with me."

"All right. Go ahead with the bath, Martha. I'll hold him until you're ready."

He waited until she was across the room before whispering next to the boy's ear. "What's your name?"

The boy burrowed further into Cole's coat, turning his head away. Rubbing his broad hand over the boy's back, he wondered what had happened for the boy to hide under the porch. Whatever the cause, it had caused a young boy to flee into freezing weather.

Shifting to look over his shoulder at Martha, he watched as she added hot water from the stove to the half full tub of cold water. When she glanced up, he smiled, getting a tentative one in return. He knew the hesitancy had a great deal to do with his lack of attention to her since returning with Dante. Cole also knew he had to make it right if he hoped to salvage a relationship with her.

"All right, partner. Miss van Plew has a bath ready for you."

When Cole didn't hear a response, he looked down at the boy.

"Are you ready for a bath?" Again, the boy didn't react to his question.

This time, Cole pulled the blanket aside. The boy was asleep, a low kitten purr breaking through his lips.

Hating to wake the boy, he cradled him in his arms while he crossed the room to the tub of warm water. Martha helped him remove the dirt-crusted clothing until they reached his loose-fitting linen drawers.

"Do you mind setting him in the tub?"

Cole grinned. "Not at all. I'll wash him and dress him in the clothes you've provided."

"Thank you. I need to check with the other children." Gabe and Beth walked into the kitchen as Martha left. Gabe stopped next to Cole while Beth headed toward the front of the house.

"Martha told us you'd discovered a boy outside. How's he doing?"

"I'm not certain. He's cold, and probably hungry."

"And asleep," Gabe noted. "Did he say anything to you?"

Cole glanced down at the still sleeping child. "Nothing. He won't tell me his name. I'm hoping once he's cleaned up, dressed, and has food in his belly, he'll be more inclined to talk." He carefully set the boy in the water, surprised when he didn't wake up.

Gabe gave a slow nod. "Maybe."

"He can't be more than five or six years old. Could be younger."

"Makes you wonder why such a young boy would run away." Gabe scratched the back of his neck. "A local family would've already reported him missing."

"Unless he ran away within the last day or two. What bothers me the most was the look in his eyes when I found him under the front porch."

The boy stirred, though he still didn't wake up. The sleep gave Cole time to wash and dry him.

"What did you mean by the look in his eyes?"

"Wild, scared. He must've been running from something awful." Cole slid clean drawers, then pants up his legs before the boy's eyes popped open. He stared from one man to the next before struggling to get out of Cole's grasp.

"Whoa, partner. There's no danger here." Cole repeated the words twice more before the boy settled down, though his eyes were still huge and fearful. "This is Sheriff Evans. Have you heard of him?"

The boy shook his head, but didn't try to get away.

"What about the town of Splendor?" Gabe asked.

Again, he shook his head. The men exchanged confused glances.

"Does your ma and pa live near Splendor?" Cole asked.

"They're dead." Those were the first words the boy had spoken.

"What's your name?"

The boy glanced away as if trying to decide if he should answer.

"Timmy?" Gabe tried. "Billy?" This time, the boy shook his head. "Then how about Finnegan?"

The boy's mouth twitched before a tiny grin appeared. "Nooo." He giggled.

"Let me think." Gabe rubbed his forehead. "I know. Charles."

The boy's face sobered, his eyes reflecting nothing of the humor from a moment earlier. "My pa was Charles."

Gabe reached out, placing a hand on the boy's shoulder. "What'd they call you?"

"Charlie."

"I'm sorry about your folks, Charlie." Gabe paused a minute before continuing. "Where have you been living?"

"My uncle. I don't like him."

"Why is that?" Cole asked.

"He's a bad man. And he's not even my uncle."

Both men raised their brows, Cole asking the next question. "If he's not your uncle, who is he?"

Charlie's mouth pinched, and his eyes narrowed when he looked at Cole. "A very bad man."

"Were you able to learn the boy's name?" Martha walked farther into the kitchen and glanced around, disappointed to find the boy and Gabe gone. "Where is he?"

Cole turned away from the window to face her. "Charlie is sleeping in a bedroom on the first floor. Gabe is checking on Beth. He asked me to stay here and keep watch toward the back."

Martha stood beside him to look through the windows, her gaze scanning the area where the children played. "I've asked Rose and Amy to bring everyone upstairs. It's time for them to be outside for a while. Unless you don't believe it's safe."

"It should be fine with Gabe, Beth, and me keeping watch."

They stood in silence for several minutes, children's voices coming from the hall as they were led outside. The kitchen windows provided them a view of the boys and girls running down the steps to the backyard, scattering to different corners.

"It's as if nothing has happened."

Cole turned to face Martha. "What do you mean?"

"Children are quite resilient. Watching them, you'd never know one of their friends was kidnapped and is still missing. I suppose it's a blessing."

"How do you figure?"

She shifted to look at him. "Well, they don't dwell on misfortune. They're better and faster at adjusting to circumstances than adults."

Cole nodded. "It's understandable. They carry no responsibility for finding Teddy or making certain it doesn't happen again."

"True. I do believe some of the older children, those closer to Teddy's age, think about him during the day. It may be they carry a fear the same will happen to them. Do you think he's still alive?"

It was a question Cole asked himself every hour of the day. "I don't want to speculate, Martha. My hope is he's being treated well."

"Though you doubt it."

"Who knows what goes on in the mind of a kidnapper? Especially one who'd kidnap a child."

"And Charlie?" Martha asked.

"What about him?"

"Perhaps he was kidnapped and ran away."

Cole had thought of the possibility. After listening to Charlie describe his circumstances, it became a strong prospect.

"He told Gabe and me his parents are dead. He's been living with an uncle." Jaw clenched, he ground out the rest. "Charlie called him a very bad man."

Chapter Seven

Northern Utah

Dorinda Heaton tugged her son, Joel, against her side, wrapping the shared blanket around them. The wagon bumped along the frozen ground as light snow continued to fall. The solid man holding the lines directed the mules over the winding trail with seasoned practice.

"Uncle Spencer?"

Spencer Haglund looked down at Joel, who sat between his mother and uncle. "Yes?"

"Why are we leaving the farm?"

Before Spencer could answer, Dorinda drew him tight against her side. "I already explained. We are visiting the ranch where Uncle Spencer works." She glanced over Joel's head with pleading eyes at her older brother.

"Just what your mother said, Joel." Spencer winked at his sister, noticing the relieved sigh. He'd already noticed how she kept glancing behind them, a mixture of fear and relief in her eyes when she found no one had followed them. He'd also noticed the formal speech common among those following the Mormon faith. In time, he knew she'd revert back to the less formal speech from her youth.

"How long until we get to the ranch?"

Spencer again looked at his nephew. "Well, Joel, longer than you'll like. Up here a ways, we'll trade this wagon in for the stagecoach to Splendor."

Crinkling his nose, Joel's gaze moved to his mother, then back at his uncle. "What is Splendor?"

"It's a town in Montana, close to the ranch where I live."

"And work?"

"That's right, Joel." Maneuvering the wagon over a mound of snow, he continued around a bend. "Look up ahead."

Peeking through an opening in the blanket, Joel sat up straighter. "We are going to the big town?"

"I have a room for us in a motel. We'll catch the stage in the morning. With luck, we'll be in Splendor in no time at all."

Dorinda's stomach refused to stop churning. She'd planned her escape carefully, yet the sense something had been overlooked haunted her.

"Do you think we will be all right spending the night in town?"

Spencer took his time responding. "We don't have a choice, Dorie. The stage is due at the station at nine in the morning. We'd miss it if we continue north. Plus..." He pointed up, into the falling snow. "It could get worse."

"Yes, you are right."

"I understand your urgency to put all of this behind you. We'll be on our way tomorrow. Until then, try not to let anyone get a good look at you or Joel."

He caught sight of his nephew, who'd been following their conversation. Spencer wondered how much the young boy knew. Maybe more than either he or Dorinda would guess.

"Mama, look there." Joel pointed out the window of the stage. A herd of elk moved across an open field, noses digging through the few inches of snow.

"We have seen those at the farm, son."

"Not that many."

A smile crossed her face. The first one since leaving the farm. "Very true."

They'd been lucky. The early winter weather had been more mild than usual. Dorinda had wanted to leave in early November, but the opportunity never came. Waiting had been the wise choice.

She checked the small watch pinned to the front of her blouse. It had belonged to her mother. Spencer carried the watch his father purchased at the end of the war between the states. Within a few years, both parents would be gone. Their father from an accident on their ranch, and their mother from cancer of the glands. One death quick, the other long and painful.

"Mama. Look there." Again, he pointed. Though the stage windows were covered with lengths of leather, they could be pulled away to look outside.

Dorinda followed his gaze. "A bear."

"It is a big one."

"Yes, it is."

Spencer sat opposite them with his hat pulled over his face. The mention of a bear had him sitting up. "It's a grizzly."

"Papa told me about them."

Dorinda stilled at the mention of her husband. In her mind, the man who'd betrayed her, ruining what she'd considered a wonderful life and marriage.

"I'm surprised he isn't hibernating in his den."

Joel's head whipped around to look at his uncle. "He?"

"That one is big. Maybe five hundred pounds. My guess is it's a male." They watched in silence until the stage had left the bear behind.

The miles passed, one after another, each one taking Dorinda farther away from the life she once believed would be hers until death. A successful farm, large house meant for many children, and a husband she loved with all her heart. She'd learned it all had been a fantasy. She looked at her brother.

"Tell us about the ranch, Spencer."

Clearing his throat, he thought a moment before responding. "It's owned by the Pelletier family. Dax and Luke came west after the war, landing in Splendor after inheriting the ranch. Redemption's Edge is the largest ranch in western Montana. Maybe in all of the territory. They run cattle and breed horses. Solid stock meant for ranch work. I work the cattle with one of the foremen. Bull Mason is one of the best men I've ever known. Same with the Pelletier brothers and most of the men at the ranch. I'm lucky they hired me."

"Are there women at the ranch?"

A chuckle burst through his lips. "Lots of women. Several of the men are married and live at the ranch." Spencer looked at his nephew. "And there are lots of children. When the weather gets too hard to take the children to school in town, the women teach them at home."

"Will we live at the ranch, Uncle Spencer?"

"You sure will. The men built a small house just for you and your mama."

Joel looked at his mother. "Just for you and me, Mama. Do I have my own bed?"

"You do. It's in your mother's bedroom, but there's a curtain you can pull around your bed," Spencer answered.

Dorinda swiped at a sudden tear. "That is so generous of the Pelletiers. I will have to find a way to thank them."

"Settle in for a bit, Dorie. There'll be plenty of time to show your gratitude."

She shifted on the uncomfortable seat. "I am surprised the stagecoaches are still traveling. I mean, the snow and ice must make it hard to move from one stop to the next."

"This may be the last run for a while. I heard there's a big storm coming this way. I'm hoping we're far enough ahead of it to get all the way to Splendor."

"And if we do not make it?" Dorinda glanced down at Joel.

"We'll find a place to wait it out." Spencer reached out, tugging the blanket under his nephew's chin, then his sister's. "Are you two warm enough?"

"We are fine, Spencer." Dorinda offered her brother a weary smile. "We are going to be just fine."

Martha hummed to herself while watching Charlie sleep. It had been two days since Cole found him hiding under the front porch. They'd learned little else from him. Until a few hours earlier.

Charlie had been sitting next to Cole at supper, shoveling food into his mouth as if he'd been starved. Maybe he had been before finding the orphanage. When finished, Charlie shared that there were two other boys living with his uncle. Plus three other men.

One boy had been with his uncle for several weeks. The other boy showed up a few days before Charlie ran away. He didn't know much about the newest boy, not even his name. It wasn't much, but might prove useful.

"How's he doing?"

Martha stopped humming to look at Cole, who stood in the doorway to the large room where all the boys slept. Charlie bunked down in the bed closest to the door, a little away from the others.

"Fine. He didn't say anything more before falling asleep. Poor thing. He's had a hard time since his parents died." Standing, she leaned down to tuck the blanket under his chin before joining Cole in the hallway.

She followed him down the stairs, continuing to the kitchen, where Beth cradled a cup of coffee. The lone female deputy looked up when they entered.

"Gabe's asleep in the living room. He plans to ride back to town in the morning."

"With you?" Cole asked.

"Yes. The other search parties were to return to town today whether they found Teddy or not. He wants to regroup, decide what to do next."

"So, he's not giving up?" Martha asked.

"Not at all. He wants to talk to Charlie before leaving. Maybe he can tell the sheriff where his uncle is holed up."

Cole shoved both hands into pockets, staring down at the floor a moment before looking back up. "He's still pretty scared. My guess is he took off without any idea the direction he was headed. I'd be surprised if he can tell us much. It's still worth asking."

Martha glanced upstairs. "Maybe you can try in the morning, Cole. He seems to trust you the most."

"I'm willing to give it a try. Is the front locked up, Beth?"

"Yes, and I've made sure all the windows and other doors are secure. Those men who came here may know the sheriff and two deputies are guarding the home. It's doubtful they'll be back as long as we're here."

Cole nodded. "You could be right. I'll stay here when you two ride off tomorrow."

"Maybe I should stay, too."

"Don't change your plans, Beth. I'll talk to Gabe about sending one or two other deputies to help me. I'd be obliged if you'd check on Dante for me."

"He's still at Gabe's house. Lena will take good care of him. Even with the age difference, Dante and Jackson get along real well. I'd planned to keep him with me and Chan. Then Gabe wanted me to help with the search." She shrugged. "I'm glad Lena volunteered to keep him."

"Thanks, Beth. I owe you."

"You don't owe me anything, Cole. It's always a pleasure to spend time with Dante."

Martha listened to the conversation, the pain in her chest increasing with each word. She couldn't stop thinking it should've been her who took care of Dante.

But Cole had cut her out of his life. She wondered if he'd ever let her back in. If she'd ever get to know Dante and the reason he'd landed in Splendor with Cole.

Chapter Eight

Dorinda could hear Joel's teeth chattering. Hers were close to doing the same. Pulling back the leather panel covering the window, she glanced outside. Other than being closer to sundown, nothing had changed in the last hour.

The storm swooped in on them several miles from Splendor, forcing the driver to stop under a canopy of tall pines. Spencer had told them they were fortunate the driver didn't have to pull off the trail. She supposed he was right. It could've been worse.

"Are there any more clothes in Joel's satchel?" Spencer asked.

She shook her head at her brother. "He is wearing everything he owns."

The driver climbed inside, bringing with him three buffalo robes. "Put these around you."

Behind him, the guard tossed in two more robes before climbing inside. "There's one more in the boot." He referred to the storage area at the back of the stage.

"There's one for each of us. That should be enough," the driver said.

The two left the relative warmth of the coach several minutes earlier to check the horses and the rigging. Both wore much warmer clothing than Dorinda had packed for her and Joel. Big men, their presence helped to warm the inside of the cab.

The driver cleared his throat. "As soon as this storm passes, we'll be on our way."

Dorinda's brows furrowed. "What about all the snow on the trail?"

"The storm isn't dumping all that much, ma'am. A few inches is all. What we have to be careful of is ice. But I've driven this stage for a few years now, in worse conditions. We'll make it to Splendor."

Dorinda didn't respond, busying herself by closing the buffalo robe around Joel. She then fidgeted with her own robe until it covered her the way she wanted.

Spencer gave the driver a supportive nod. "You know your job. We trust you to get us to Splendor."

The coach quieted, everyone seeming to listen for any change in the storm. What they heard was...nothing.

The driver threw off the buffalo robe. "This may be our chance. Just stay where you are and we'll get this rig moving."

The guard followed the driver outside. Several minutes passed before the stage rocked when the two climbed up top. Slapping the lines, the coach jerked forward, then backward, before the horses broke it from the ice and started on the trail.

Joel fell asleep soon afterward. Dorinda kept her arm around him, knowing she wouldn't sleep until they reached Splendor.

"Are you doing all right, Dorie?"

She nodded at her brother. "I haven't thanked you for all you've done."

"No need. I know you've been miserable since Jared took a second wife." Spencer gave a slow shake of his head. "Never thought he'd do it. Not even with all the pressure from the elders. I thought he'd promised you to never take more wives."

"He did."

"What's done is done, Dorie. No reason to ever bring it up again."

Her heart squeezed, throat tightened, making it difficult to reply. "Thank you." Her voice was no more than a whisper.

The stagecoach rocked, making a slow turn to the right before stopping. Dorinda pulled back the leather flap to look outside, seeing almost total darkness. Her brows drew together in a frown.

"I do not see any buildings."

Spencer removed the buffalo robe. "Stay in here."

Outside, he saw a large house with a few lights on inside. "What's that?" he asked the driver.

"Orphanage. I'm going to ask Miss van Plew if we can stay until morning." Climbing down, he adjusted his pants. "The horses, well, they aren't going to make it to town."

"How far is it?"

"In good weather, about fifteen minutes. Longer with the snow."

Spencer glanced around. "They got more than we did where we stopped."

"Quite a bit. Well, I'd better talk to Miss van Plew."

Spencer watched until he knocked on the front door, then poked his head into the stagecoach. Explaining what was happening, he studied Dorinda's face.

"You need sleep."

She offered an exhausted smile. "We all do."

"We're welcome inside." The driver's breaths came in short gasps from walking in the snow. "I'll get your bags from up top. Don't want them to disappear during the night."

Spencer helped his sister roust Joel, then lifted him into his arms. "Easier than trying to get him to walk in the snow."

"Should we bring the buffalo robes inside?"

He shook his head. "I'll come back and get them if it's not warm enough inside."

It took more energy than Dorinda expected to take the steps to the front door. A tall woman greeted them, motioning them toward the kitchen.

"I'm sure you're hungry. There's plenty of stew left. I hope that'll be all right."

"It's more than we planned," Spencer answered. "Is there a place I can lay down my nephew?"

"There's a bedroom with two beds upstairs. It should be big enough for all three of you. Follow me."

"No need for you to go, ma'am. Just tell me which bedroom."

Martha explained. "I'll warm up the stew and cornbread." She cocked her head to the side. "Have we met? You look familiar."

"I'm Spencer Haglund. I work at the Pelletier ranch. One of my jobs is to fetch supplies from town."

"Oh, I remember you now. You helped me load my purchases at the general store into our wagon. It wasn't that long ago."

"I remember you, Miss van Plew. It was a week or so before Thanksgiving."

"That's right. It's nice to have the chance to help you." Smiling, she turned toward the kitchen.

Dorinda, the driver, and the guard were already warming themselves by the large cookstove when Martha entered. "It'll be just a few minutes before the food is warm."

"We appreciate this, Miss van Plew," Dorinda said. She introduced herself.

A tall man with an olive complexion walked in from the hall, removing his hat. A star was pinned to his coat.

"This is Deputy Santori." Martha took a minute to introduce the guests and explain his presence. "Cole, how about some coffee?"

"I'd appreciate it." Setting his hat on a hook, he took a seat at a long table in the kitchen. The others joined him. "Storm must've hit you pretty hard."

The driver nodded. "It did. Decided we couldn't make it to Splendor. The stage company won't like it, but it was the right thing to do."

"It would take a good half hour to reach Splendor," Cole said. "That assumes the storm doesn't get worse." He looked at Dorinda.

"Where are you headed, Mrs. Heaton?"

"My son and I plan to settle in Splendor. For now, we will stay at the Pelletier ranch. My brother works there."

"That right? What's his name?"

"Evening, Cole." Spencer appeared from the hall. "I see you've met my sister."

Cole stood, accepting the outstretched hand. "Spencer. So, this is your sister."

He nodded. "Dorinda, this is one of the best lawmen in these parts." He took a seat next to her. "What brings you to the orphanage?"

Cole explained about the kidnapped boy and how several search parties had returned without finding him. "Even our best trackers couldn't find a single sign." He then explained about Charlie.

"Do you think the man he ran from is connected to the missing boy?" Spencer asked.

"I wouldn't be surprised."

Dorinda saw Martha carry bowls to a table next to the cookstove and rose. "May I help you?"

"I'd appreciate it." She ladled stew into two bowls, handing them to Dorinda. When she returned, Martha handed her two more, carrying the last bowl herself. She placed it in front of Cole. "I'll get the cornbread."

Everyone waited until she set the plate of already cut cornbread on the table. "Please, go ahead."

They dug into the food as if they hadn't eaten in days. Other than jerky, hardtack, and coffee, they hadn't.

"This is wonderful," Dorinda said between bites.

"We make huge pots of stew. The cold weather makes it easy, as we put what's left in covered pans outside." Martha sipped coffee as the others ate.

"How long have you been working here?" Dorinda asked.

Martha chuckled. "Well, it's more a labor of love than a job. I'm part of a group of women who decided a home was necessary. We found this abandoned house, negotiated a fair price with the bank, and raised money to purchase it. Most of the work to repair the house was organized by Noah Brandt, one of the town leaders. He donated much of the labor. Silas Jenks, who owns the lumber mill, donated most of the lumber for repairs. Townsfolk showed up to help. It's been a remarkable experience."

"Martha is the administrator until the committee locates a suitable replacement." Cole looked at her over his cup of coffee.

They talked about the children living at the home, their activities, and about other children attending school with the orphans. "The town leaders are searching for a new teacher for those who aren't orphaned. We're hoping to hire someone before the end of the year."

Dorinda slid her bowl away. "Does not give you much time."

"No, but I'm hopeful. We've received several inquiries from both men and women. None of them worked out. It's not easy to leave a big city for the frontier of Montana. We'll have more success with someone familiar with life in a small town."

Dorinda recalled her time assisting the teacher near their farm in Utah. The one room schoolhouse held twenty-five children of different ages. She loved the work. When Dorinda discovered she was with child, Jared had insisted she quit.

A child screaming had all the adults jumping to their feet. Cole drew his six-shooter as he ran to the steps. The scream came again from upstairs. He took the steps two at a time, reaching the landing as a figure dressed in black climbed out a window.

"Stop!"

The figure paid no attention to Cole's command. Dorinda followed Spencer up the stairs and into the bedroom where Joel had been asleep. Rushing to the bed, she wrapped her arms around her son. He stared straight ahead and continued to scream.

Chapter Nine

Cole and Spencer ran outside. They hoped to stop the intruder as he hit the ground. Rounding the corner of the house, they looked around, spotting the figure dressed in black disappearing into the trees. The whinnying of a horse came seconds later.

"No use following tonight. It'll be too dark to spot the tracks." Cole slammed his six-shooter into the holster. "We almost had him."

"Did you see his face?"

"No, but I'm certain it was a man. Could be the same one who took Teddy."

Spencer shifted to take another look around before holstering his gun. "You stopped him from taking Joel."

"Joel's screams saved him."

Spencer chuckled. "That boy does have a set of lungs." He holstered his gun. "You know, he took quite a chance entering the house with a lawman inside."

"You're right. Could be we aren't dealing with a real smart kidnapper. I wonder if it was Charlie's uncle." Cole turned back toward the front steps. "Or could've been the man who took Teddy. I suppose they could be one and the same. He just walked into the wrong bedroom. Martha's probably busy calming the orphans."

"What are your plans, Cole?" They stopped at the bottom of the steps.

"I'll ride into Splendor tomorrow morning to let Gabe know what we saw."

"I'm riding in on the stage. I'll tell him."

"I'd appreciate it, Spencer. That way Martha and the children won't be left without protection."

The stage driver intercepted them before they were five feet inside. "The women are upstairs with the children."

"Best to let them take care of it." Cole hung his hat on hooks by the front door. Spencer did the same.

He walked through the house to the back door, glad Spencer had followed. "I want to see how the man got upstairs. The window should've been locked."

Cole didn't have to wonder long. A ladder had been placed under the window. Neither man commented.

"A ladder and open window." Spencer continued to stare upward, rubbing his chin.

"I'll talk to Martha about double-checking the windows each night. Whoever is doing this isn't going to give up."

"Not until they're caught," Spencer said.

Cole let out a deep breath. One he'd been holding for too long. "Right."

The coach stopped in the thick mud in front of the stagecoach station. Jumping down, the driver checked the office door. Locked. He'd known when they'd left the orphanage the stage would arrive before Bernie Griggs opened for business.

"He's not here, but you can get out."

By the time the driver and guard unloaded the luggage from atop the stage, Dorinda, Joel, and Spencer were standing on the boardwalk. Most businesses hadn't opened.

"The boardinghouse is open." Spencer nodded. "We'll get breakfast, then I'll arrange for a wagon to take us out to Redemption's Edge."

"I want pancakes, Mama."

"Suzanne makes the best in town." Spencer surveyed the deep mud between them and the restaurant.

"I will carry Joel across," Dorinda said.

"I am big. I can go across by myself." The indignance in his voice had both adults smiling.

"You are," Spencer said. "The problem is you'd get swallowed up. Probably lose your boots. Come on, I'll take you across before helping your ma." He held out his arms.

Joel hesitated an instant. He stared at the street, then looked at Spencer. Making up his mind, he walked into his uncle's arms. Leaving Joel in front of the restaurant, he returned for Dorinda.

"I can walk."

"Sure you can." He looked down at boots soaked in sticky mud. "No sense both of us getting this on your dress. You'd probably lose your boots in the middle of the street." Giving no warning, he scooped his sister into his arms and started across.

"Our bags?"

"I'll go back for them. You head inside with Joel and get warm. Order me coffee, eggs, bacon, potatoes, and hotcakes."

Dorinda rushed Joel into the restaurant the instant Spencer set her down. The inside was warm and welcoming. Half the tables were already being used, which left several to choose from.

"We will take the table by the window, Joel." The words had barely left her mouth before he hurried across the room to the table.

"I have it, Mama."

Several patrons laughed while most of the others smiled at the boy's loud voice. He didn't even notice.

Feeling her face flush, she joined Joel. "You did real good."

Beaming, he wrestled with the chair before jumping onto it. "Where did Uncle Spencer go?"

"He is getting us a wagon."

"Good morning. You two must be new to town. I'm Suzanne and I own this place."

"Yes, we are new. I am Dorinda Heaton and this is my son, Joel."

"Well, I'm glad to meet you. Do you know what you want?"

"Pancakes."

"We definitely have plenty of those, young man. And for you?"

"A fried egg and toast. Milk for both of us, please. Oh, and I need to order for my brother." Dorinda recited what he'd said. "He eats a lot."

"Oh, that's not so much. Most of the men around here have big appetites. Is your brother new, also?"

"No. He works for the Pelletiers. We will live at their ranch for a while."

"They're wonderful people. And there are a number of women and children. Who's your brother?"

"Spencer Haglund."

"Spencer? He comes in after church on Sundays. Real nice man."

"Yes, he is."

"I'll get your food out right away."

Dorinda watched Suzanne walk away, wondering at the reference to a church. Spencer had left the Mormon faith, and Utah, not long after their parents moved south to New Mexico with several other families at the request of their bishop. He'd never mentioned another church in his letters.

"It's getting colder out there." Spencer's voice drew her attention. "Noah Brandt had a wagon available."

The table fell into silence. Even after Suzanne brought their meals, they didn't talk.

Dorinda had so many questions for Spencer. Most she wouldn't ask in front of Joel. Maybe at the ranch, they'd have time to talk.

Orphanage

"I'm glad you stayed, Cole. The three of us can keep watch, but your presence is a better deterrent." Martha stood next to him on the back porch, holding out a cup of coffee.

"Thank you." Their eyes met and held a moment longer than necessary when he took the cup from her hand. Taking a sip, he watched her over the brim before turning his attention back to the children.

"The snow is melting. Soon, everyone will be covered in a mixture of mud and melted snow. Laundry takes up a large amount of our time. I do most of it."

"Why is that?" He took another sip.

"Amy and Rose weren't hired on to do housekeeping and laundry. They never complain," Martha added. "Still, it's best if I do a major portion of the chores until we hire someone."

"When will that be?"

"Soon, I hope." The last was said with a chuckle. "We had a wonderful woman for the first two months. Her husband found work in Big Pine, so they left."

"Ah." He nodded.

When neither spoke for a few minutes, she ventured into the question festering for a while. "Who is Dante?"

Brows furrowed, he looked at her. "My son." He blew out a breath. "My adopted son."

"I see."

The corners of Cole's mouth tipped up, though his eyes showed no trace of humor. "It's a long story, Martha." He stared down at his boots a moment before meeting her gaze. "I should've told you a long time ago. When we came back to Splendor."

"What stopped you?"

"I don't know. The timing never quite worked out. Gabe offered me work during the week, with nights and weekends off. It's the same as he offers any of his deputies who have a family. He's especially considerate of those who don't have a wife."

"So you drop him off in the morning and head to town. Then you pick him up in the afternoon and return to town so you can finish your duties. Who watches him?"

"Part of the time, I work at the jail. Dante stays with me. He completes any schoolwork sent home. He stays with a widow woman in town on the other days."

"I see. Well, I suppose it's time for me to finish my chores." She turned to leave, stopping when he grabbed her arm.

"Wait. Please."

She turned back toward him. "Yes?"

"It was wrong of me to avoid talking to you, Martha. You deserved better."

She scoffed. "Yes, I did deserve better. All the same, I'm glad you've found a good woman who's willing to watch Dante."

Her meaning sank in about the time she turned away. "Wait, Martha."

"Not now, Cole. I do have to get on with my chores if I'm going to finish them before the children come back inside."

"You don't understand."

"There's no misunderstanding."

He opened his mouth to respond when shouting from the backyard drew their attention. Handing his empty cup to Martha, he rushed outside to the children shouting. Amy and Rose were already with them, looking around.

"What's going on?"

A girl pointed toward a cluster of dense bushes. Her breath came in gasps. "Over there. Two men were watching us."

"Maybe three," a boy said.

"I only saw two," the girl responded.

"All right." Cole bent down. "There were two or three men in those bushes watching you. What else did either of you see?"

The boy and girl exchanged glances.

"Nothing else," the girl said.

"Did you get a good look at them?"

"Nah. But they were men," the boy said.

"Have either of you seen them around here before?"

The two shook their heads.

He straightened. "How about the rest of you? Any of you see the men today or earlier?"

Some shook their heads while others continued to stare at him. He looked at Martha. "Might be time to bring the children inside."

"Of course." Martha nodded at Amy and Rose, who accompanied the children into the house. When she went to follow, he again stopped her.

"We have to talk, Martha. You need to let me explain."

"There's a lot going on right now, Cole. It might be best to let it go for now. At least until we discover what happened to Teddy."

He took a step closer. "I don't want to put it off much longer."

"And I'm not ready to hear your story. Not today anyway." Shaking her head, Martha walked back into the house, leaving Cole alone, watching her leave.

Chapter Ten

Cole heard the horses first.

Riders approached from the north. More than one, if his hearing was sound. He expected to see Gabe and his deputies, reminding himself it could be the kidnappers or the three men who'd bothered Martha.

The children and Rose were in the classroom with Martha while Amy prepared lunch for everyone. With no time to alert them, he took a position on the front porch. His rifle leaned against the wall near the front door. He grabbed it, preferring the long-range gun to his six-shooter.

Spotting the riders, he lifted the rifle to his shoulder before he recognized Gabe in the front. Lowering the gun, he set it down. He counted eight riders, including Noah Brandt and Bull Mason, one of the foremen at the Pelletier ranch.

All were bundled against the cold, which had dropped overnight. Turning up the collar of his coat, he walked down the steps to meet them.

Gabe dismounted first, followed by Noah, Bull, and deputies Dutch, Shane, Morgan, Jonas, and Tucker. Dutch's appearance surprised Cole, as he'd taken time away to visit a woman in Big Pine.

"Morning, gents."

"Spencer told me what happened here. Did he try to break in again?" Gabe pulled off his gloves, following Cole inside. The others weren't far behind.

"No. There was an instance yesterday where two of the children spotted two or three men hiding in the bushes. They took off, and haven't returned. Cowards," Cole scoffed. "What's your plan?" He headed into the kitchen.

"Let's discuss what to do next over coffee."

"I'll make more. Amy has four coffeepots in the cupboards. Shouldn't take long, as we're keeping the stove stoked."

At the mention of Amy, Morgan looked up from where he leaned against a wall. Cole had heard the deputy held an interest in her. Morgan cleared his throat.

"Where are the women?" Morgan asked. Jonas and Tucker snickered, shooting their friend knowing looks.

"Amy should be here somewhere. She may be in the root cellar. Rose and Martha are in the classroom with the children. That reminds me, Gabe. Are you still holding off bringing the children from town until we find Teddy?"

"For now. With the weather and Christmas coming up, I may ask Ruth Paige if she'd be willing to hold school in the community building. I'd rather find Teddy and arrest anyone connected to the kidnapping."

Morgan cleared his throat a second time. "Uh, maybe I should check on Amy. She might need help."

"Go on then." Gabe hid his smirk, as did the others. "Get back here as soon as you find her."

"Yes, sir."

When the outside door closed, Gabe looked at Cole. "I'd like Tucker and Jonas to speak with Charlie. They're younger than us. Maybe he'll open up to them, remember more than what he's given us so far."

Removing his hat, Tucker scratched the back of his neck. "I don't know, Gabe. You told us the boy is five. I'm twenty-five and Jonas is twenty-four. That's old to a young boy."

"You're the best chance we have." Gabe shifted his attention back to Cole. "Unless one of the older orphan boys is willing to help us."

"We should talk to Martha about this."

"Talk to me about what?"

The men stood when Martha joined them. "Ma'am," they said in unison.

"Please, sit down. Sheriff, I hoped we'd see you today. So, tell me what you're planning."

Gabe explained. "What do you think?"

She thought for a bit before answering. "The boy everyone respects lives in town. I believe Charlie might open up to him."

"I'll send Tucker and Jonas to fetch him. Who is it?"

"It's your son, Jackson."

"Doggone it, Doubt. I told you we shoulda grabbed more boys before Sheriff Evans returned with his deputies." Hammer stared at the leader of the outlaw gang while warming himself at the old stove in the dilapidated cabin. He glanced across the room where two boys huddled together.

Doubt Bergstrom stopped pacing, his voice low and menacing. "We tried twice to take another boy. Two of the brats spotted us in the bushes, and the other...well, you know how that turned out since you were the one who had to scramble through the window. You swore this would be easy. Grab a few boys, sell them to the Mexicans, and move on."

Hammer scratched his stubbled jaw. "Guess I was wrong."

Both turned toward the door as two more men entered. Doubt and Hammer acknowledged them with nods.

"Dang it, Hammer. What are we gonna do? Charlie ran away. That leaves us with Teddy and the boy we picked up on the streets of Big Pine."

"Joey," Hammer said.

"Right. Joey and Teddy are all we got. How many boys did you tell Gonzales we'd fetch for him?"

"We settled on six."

"Four more." Doubt said the number as if it were a curse. "Might as well be twenty."

"We could never handle that many."

Doubt looked at the other two men, then back at Hammer, shaking his head. The scruffy twins stared at the two men who stood a couple feet apart. "I know that."

"So what are we going to do?"

"We're going after two more boys. We'll offer the four to Gonzales. I guarantee he won't turn us away."

"I don't know, Doubt. Gonzales expects six. We show up with four, well, I just don't know."

"Trust me. I know. We're going to snatch two more. Then we'll ride straight to Gonzales' camp." Doubt shot an assessing look at the twins, who sat next to each other on the only bed. "This time, all four of us go."

"No, no, no. You aren't using the boys as bait." Martha glared at Gabe, her jaw set. "If anything went wrong..." She let out a shaky breath.

"There are a total of nine men, Martha. They'll be spaced around the backyard and front of the house. You've got five boys, including Charlie. We'll protect them."

She glanced at Cole. "I can't lose any more of the children."

"Gabe is right. All of us, except Noah and Bull, are trained lawmen. And I'd take those two with me into battle any day." Rising, he moved to the kitchen window. The other men were scattered around the backyard, guarding the children as they played. "Gabe's plan is the best way to end this and get Teddy back."

Her back straight, shoulders square in a position Cole had seen many times in the women of his family, he waited for Martha to speak. He knew how much she cared about the children, treating them as if they were her own. In many ways, they were.

"You're certain this is the only way, Gabe?"

"We know the kidnappers want more children. Our search parties have turned up nothing. This is the only way I know to draw them to us. We'll be careful. The children will be safe."

"Gabe. Tucker and Jonas are returning with Jackson." Noah stood in the doorway, his knowing gaze boring into the man who'd been his best friend since they were children in New York. He turned at the sound of footfalls in the living room.

"Uncle Noah. I didn't know you'd be here." Jackson stopped next to him, his eyes widening when he spotted his father. "Hey, Papa. Miss van Plew."

She smiled at him.

"Hey, Jack. Did Tucker and Jonas tell you what's going on?"

The boy nodded, his features turning serious. "Somebody took Teddy. There's another boy you want me to talk to."

"He's five. Name is Charlie. We think he knows more about the kidnappers. One of them is his uncle."

Jackson walked to the table where Gabe sat with Martha, his brows scrunched together. "He ran away from his uncle?"

"Seems so. We want you to talk with Charlie. Maybe he'll share more information than what he's given us."

"Sure, Papa. Where is he?"

"I'll show you." Martha stood, looking at Gabe. "I guess we don't have much choice but to go with your plan. Come on, Jackson. Charlie is upstairs."

Gabe didn't wait to put the plan in place. While Jackson met with Charlie, he and Cole went outside to speak with the other men. By the time Jackson returned, with Charlie trailing behind, the men were ready.

Jackson walked straight to his father. "Charlie says there are four men, one of them is his uncle."

Gabe looked at Charlie, who nodded.

"He also said there are two boys still at the cabin."

"Does he remember where they're holding the boys?"

Jackson shook his head.

Gabe rubbed his chin, turning toward his men. "All right. We're watching for four men. If our plan works, we'll have to get one of them to tell us where they're holding two boys." He shifted back to Jackson. "Thanks, son." He smiled at Charlie. "You were real brave to tell Jackson about the men."

Charlie acted as if he wasn't going to talk, then he opened his mouth. "They're very bad men."

"Yes, they are. But we're going to take care of them and find where they're holding Teddy and the other boy. Jackson, I want you to stay close to Charlie."

"Sure, Papa."

"Martha, how about we get these children fed? I'll explain to them what we plan while they eat."

"All right." She ushered the children inside.

While they ate, Gabe and his men finalized how they'd implement the plan. They were ready to head inside to eat when a rider galloped toward them from the east.

"It's Bull," Noah said.

The ranch foreman reined his horse to a stop within a few feet of the men. "Riders coming from the east. I counted four."

"How fast are they moving?" Gabe asked.

"Real slow," Bull answered.

Gabe looked at the assembled group and smiled. "Time to put our plan into action."

Chapter Eleven

"You sure this is how you want to do this, Doubt? Don't think it's going to work out well for us."

The group had pulled up on a small rise not far from the orphanage. They'd left Teddy and the other boy behind, their hands and ankles bound. Doubt shot a disgusted glance at Hammer.

"You think too much, Hammer. Doesn't sit well with you."

"I'm serious about waiting."

"We should've done this before now."

"Dang it, Doubt. They've got more men guarding the children. Maybe twice as many men as us."

From their spot on the hill, they had a decent view of the orphanage in the distance. They could see the children running down the steps into the back area. Doubt believed no one from below could see them.

"Appears they've got four deputies spread out," Doubt said.

"There were more than four when the sheriff and his men arrived."

"Don't matter, Hammer. They don't know we're coming. We catch them by surprise, snatch two boys, and ride off."

Hammer's jaw moved, but he didn't respond right away. He watched the children and deputies spread out behind the house. His stomach clenched.

"I don't like it, Doubt."

"You got a better plan?"

Hammer shook his head.

"Didn't think so." Doubt looked past Hammer to the twins. "You ready?"

The bearded, red-haired men nodded.

"All right. Let's grab us a couple more boys."

Bull put down the binoculars. He'd been posted at a window on the second floor, watching for the four men to come into sight. Across the hall, Noah did the same, looking to the west before moving to a window at the front of the house. He spotted the same four men stopped on the hill. Lowering the binoculars, he joined Bull.

"You see them?"

Bull nodded. "Four men. They appear to be looking at the orphanage."

"And the men and children out back," Noah said.

"I believe you're right. I'll stay if you'll let Gabe know."

Noah left the room, hurrying down the stairs to the back porch. Using his own binoculars, the sheriff watched the area beyond where the children played.

"They're sitting on the top of a hill in the distance. Watching the same as we're watching them. Except they don't know we've got them in our sights."

Lowering the binoculars, Gabe turned toward him. "I sure hope this works."

"It will. We'll know where they're coming from. The deputies will know when they make their move."

Gabe nodded. "You remember the hand signals we used when we were boys?"

"I do."

"Have Bull continue watching from the east bedroom. When he tells you they're making their move, you signal me from the window on the south side of the house. I'll be positioned out there." He pointed to a stand of trees which identified the outside boundary of where the children played.

Noah gave a mock salute before disappearing inside.

Gabe headed down the steps, stopping to explain their duties to each of his men. Half would keep watching the children while staying aware of the area beyond. The other half would disperse around the perimeter, acting as if they were watching the children while focusing on the area beyond. Dutch was the last man he spoke to, a person with an uncanny sense of an action before it happened.

"We'll get those miscreants, Gabe. Don't you worry."

Looking around, he surveyed the position of each deputy. Lifting his gaze, he spotted Noah in the window. He gave an almost imperceptible nod, which his friend returned.

"Noah," Bull called. "They're riding down the hill toward us."

Noah appeared in the bedroom doorway. "They keeping together?"

"Sure are."

Heading back to the west bedroom, Noah leaned out, getting Gabe's attention. He gave a hand signal. Gabe nodded, alerting the deputies the kidnappers were on the move.

He spotted Martha standing next to Cole on the back porch. Gabe offered a nod, indicating the men were close. Even from the distance across the yard, he saw her take a deep, shaky breath. He knew she wouldn't leave the porch. She needed to see what occurred when the men arrived to take the children.

Another signal from Noah triggered a round of communication with the deputies. The riders were about a mile out.

The four spotters shifted positions so they weren't as visible, though they continued to give the appearance of watching the children. In reality, all the deputies guarded the children while being aware of movement in the bushes and trees.

Noah signaled again, letting Gabe know the riders were a hundred yards away. They didn't dismount as they rode closer. Without giving himself away, he shifted to get a better view. He spotted the four horses moving within the cover of the bushes and trees.

From his position, it appeared they were spreading out, putting several yards between them. The same as a lantern brightened a room, a light flashed in Gabe's mind. He knew what they planned.

Motioning for Noah to join them, he walked to another of his men. He explained what he believed the kidnappers would do before moving to another of his men. Shane Banderas snickered.

"If you're right, those boys out there are idiots."

Gabe stifled a chuckle. "I never thought they were smart."

"If that's their plan, it's insane. I won't say anymore. It makes as much sense as anything else." Shane's gaze moved over the shrubbery before settling back on Gabe. "I'll be ready."

Clasping him on the shoulder, Gabe moved on. He knew at any moment, the men hiding in the brush would make their move.

"There must be ten men out there, Doubt. We don't stand a chance of grabbing two boys and getting away."

Doubt shot a disgusted look at Hammer. "We've gone over this a hundred times. The twins will distract the men while you grab one boy and I take another. Instead of turning around, we'll keep on going, and the twins will follow."

"Then what?"

"Dang, Hammer. Weren't you listening earlier?" Doubt shook his head. "All right. I'll say this one more time. We'll ride out in a wide arc south, then head north to the cabin, where we'll haul out the other boys and head for Wyoming. Are we square now?"

"Sure, Doubt. We're square."

"Finally." He looked at the twins. "Are you two ready to ride?"

They nodded.

"Hammer?"

"Suppose I am, Doubt." Though his voice didn't include much enthusiasm.

Doubt sat straight in the saddle, jaw jutting out. Raising a fist into the air, he nudged his horse forward.

"Let's ride!"

Gabe and his men heard the horse hoofs slamming on the frozen ground before spotting the four horses charging toward them. Reflecting on it later over coffee, only those who'd fought in the war had ever witnessed anything like it.

Gabe didn't need to shout an order. His men knew where to position themselves and what he expected.

They charged from the trees, two riding toward the men who stood on the perimeter of the area where the children played. The other two rode straight at the cluster of boys and girls, who now moved toward the house.

The riders held no guns as they yipped and yelled in an attempt to create chaos. It might've worked if Gabe hadn't been expecting them. Of course, he hadn't thought they'd make such a ridiculous move against so many armed men.

Watching from the porch, he saw two riders attempt to scatter his deputies. To their credit, his men didn't draw their weapons or give up their positions. Not even when the would-be kidnappers rode in circles around them.

Noah joined him on the porch, his head tilted to one side. "What the heck are those men doing?"

"I suspect they're trying to distract our men while their partners grab one or two of the boys."

The words were just out of Gabe's mouth when the children pounded up the steps and ran into the house. Noah and Gabe watched as they disappeared inside.

"Don't believe that's going to work," Noah said.

"I believe you're right."

The battle between deputies on the ground and four horsemen lasted a few minutes. Slowing until Doubt and his boys accepted they'd lost their fight to steal more children.

Bull joined Gabe and Noah on the porch. "This has been real entertaining."

Without being ordered, Gabe's men grabbed the reins of each horse before tugging Doubt and the others to the ground. Sputtering as they lay face down in the snow and ice while Morgan, Jonas, Tucker, Cole, and Dutch secured them with handcuffs.

"They never drew their weapons," Bull said.

"It is interesting," Noah said.

"An entirely inept attempt to take the children." Gabe rubbed his chin. "At least I believe that was the reason they rode in the way they did." He motioned for Cole to join them on the porch.

"Yes, sir?"

"Go get Charlie from the boys' bunkroom. I want to see if he can identify his uncle and any of the other men."

"I'll go upstairs with you, Cole," Martha said from her spot in the doorway.

It took several minutes of coaxing to convince Charlie he'd be safe. The wide eyes and fear on his face almost had Martha deciding she should hold him back.

All the way down the stairs and through the kitchen, Martha worried about Charlie facing his uncle. "I hope we're doing the right thing," she whispered to Cole when Charlie stopped at the top of the steps.

"He'll be safe with us," he whispered back. Reaching out, he took Charlie's hand in his. "Let's go down to the yard so you can get a good look."

"But I don't need to get closer. My uncle is the closest to us."

"What's his name?"

"Doubt Bergstrom."

"Doubt?"

"Uh-huh. My mama said it was short for Doubtful. Mr. Hammer is next to him."

Cole had already recognized the outlaw, but let Charlie continue.

"Those men out there," he pointed to the two closest to the brush, "Uncle Doubt called them the twins. I don't know their names."

When the deputies tugged Doubt to his feet, Charlie flinched. "Don't let him take me."

"You're safe with us," Cole said.

Then Doubt spotted Charlie. His face twisted in rage. "You!" He almost pulled free of the hold the deputies had on him.

Staring in horror, Charlie turned and ran into the house.

Chapter Twelve

Martha followed Charlie upstairs, finding him huddled against the wall at the head of his bed. The other children emerged from the house to watch as Gabe's deputies rode to Splendor with their prisoners.

Cole sat on the end of Charlie's bed, listening as Martha calmed the scared child. He hoped the boy would be able to tell him where Teddy and the other boy were being held.

"Deputy Cole has some questions for you, Charlie. It's important you answer him as best as you can. Can you do that?"

Charlie looked at her, then at Cole, then back at Martha. "Is he gone?"

"Your uncle?"

He nodded, seeming to turn even further into himself.

"Yes," Martha said. "The deputies and the four men are gone."

Charlie's shoulders relaxed, as did the rest of his small body. "Are you going to find the boys and bring them here?"

"Yes," Martha answered. "First, we need your help to find them."

"They're in the cabin where we lived."

"Could you find it again?" Cole leaned toward him.

Charlie shook his head.

"We know you came from the east. That way." Cole pointed. "Can you remember anything unusual on your trip here?"

Scrunching his brows together, he shook his head.

"Big rocks, unusual trees, cattle, people, anything that might help us find the cabin?"

He began to shake his head again, then stopped. "A big rock with black on it."

"Black?"

"Uh-huh. It was real big, and one side was black."

Cole looked at Martha. "Do you know where he's talking about?"

She shook her head. "No, I don't."

"Charlie, was there anything else around the big rock?"

"Trees. They were black, too."

"A fire?" Martha asked Cole.

"Could be. I don't recall a big one. We would've seen it in Splendor."

"One tree looked like a spear."

Cole looked at Charlie. "Was it a tall or short spear?"

"Really tall. And black. It was close to the big rock."

"All right. Martha, could we talk in the hall?"

"Will you be all right here, Charlie?" she asked.

"Uh-huh."

Leaving the door to the bunkroom open, Martha stopped in front of Cole. "What is it?"

"Gabe, Noah, and Bull are still here. I think Jackson stayed behind, also. He had good luck getting some information out of Charlie earlier."

"You're thinking he might learn more than we've gotten?"

"It's a thought."

Martha smiled. "A good one. You bring him up and I'll let Charlie know. He seems to trust Jackson."

Several minutes later, Jackson walked past Martha, who stood in the hall, and entered the bedroom. "Hi, Charlie."

"Hi."

"Is it all right if we talk again?"

Charlie gave a slow nod. "You can sit down."

"All right." Jackson sat down near him.

Cole leaned against the hallway wall, arms crossed. Martha stood next to him, lines of worry etched on her face. She leaned closer to Cole.

"I hope Jackson is able to get more out of him," she whispered.

"Charlie's trying. The boy was scared and running for his life when he came upon the orphanage. I'm surprised he remembered the rock and trees. Those may be good enough if we can convince him to go with us."

"I doubt he'll leave without Jackson."

Cole turned this over in his head. "We'll take Jackson with us."

"Take me where?" He joined them in the hall.

"To find the other boys," Cole said. "Are you willing to go with us and Charlie?"

"I'd like to ride along. Is my father going?"

"Him, Noah, and Bull, plus you, Charlie, and me."

Jackson nodded. "Charlie told me some things that may help find Teddy and the other boy."

Martha let out a long breath. "That's wonderful. There are only a few hours until sunset. I'll get him bundled up so you can leave as soon as everyone else is ready." She looked at Cole, a smile of hope appearing on her face.

"We'll find them, Martha. No matter what, we'll bring those boys home."

"This trip would've been a lot easier if one of those miscreants had talked." Bull rode next to Cole, keeping his voice low. Behind them, Noah rode with Charlie while Jackson rode with Gabe.

"You're right. Not much we could do when all four refused to speak," Cole said. "They didn't offer any information, even when being told they could hang if either of those boys died."

"I sure hope they're sent away for a long time."

"There. Up there!" Charlie pointed ahead to a large, blackened boulder next to a grouping of burned trees.

"Do we keep going straight ahead?" Noah asked Charlie.

"I think so."

Noah looked at the others. "Let's keep going and hope Charlie recognizes something else."

A mile later, Cole shifted to look behind him at Charlie. "Does anything around here look familiar?"

"No." Then his eyes lit up. "There!"

"What are you pointing at, son?" Noah asked.

"The tree with the Christmas star on top."

Everyone raised their faces. Sure enough, they were riding straight toward one of the tallest trees around. The green foliage at the top had been replaced with what appeared to be a nest. From where they rode, it looked just like a star. A Christmas star.

"I told you this was a stupid idea, didn't I?" Hammer sat in the jail, looking at the twins in the cell next to his.

"He did tell you that, Doubt," one of the twins answered.

"He surely did," the other one said, his gaze focused on the floor of his cell. "A real stupid idea."

"It could've worked if you two had done what you were supposed to," Doubt said from the next cell.

"We did everything you said, Doubt." He looked at his twin. "Didn't we?"

His brother gave an exaggerated nod. "Exactly what Doubt told us."

Hammer looked at the twins, then Doubt. "You shoulda listened to what I told you, Doubt."

Doubt's face reddened. "What did you ever tell me that was right?"

"I said we shoulda gone in there at night. You and me, to grab two more boys. We'd have been on our way to

Wyoming if you'd listened." Hammer rested his back against the back wall of the jail.

"He's right, Doubt," one of the twins said. "You shoulda listened to Hammer."

"None of you know what you're talking about." Standing, Doubt gripped the cell bars. "Hey! When are we going to get some food?"

"Yeah!" one of the twins shouted. "We're hungry in here."

"Heck, we shouldn't even be in here."

Doubt looked through the bars at Hammer. "You don't know half of what you're yakking about."

"Know a lot more than you," Hammer shot back.

"Enough!" Deputy Hawke DeBell sauntered toward the cells. "You boys have been ruining my peace for an hour. It's time for all of you to keep your mouths shut." When Hawke turned to leave, one of the twins jumped up and grabbed the bars.

"What about our food?"

"It'll be here when Miss Suzanne has it ready. Geez. One would think you boys have never eaten."

"It's been hours," the other twin shouted when Hawke turned away a second time.

Hands on hips, the deputy shook his head as he returned to the desk. Resting his arms on top, he stared at Shane, who sat across from him.

"Were they like this on the ride back from the orphanage?"

"About the same. Never did find a way to shut them up."

The door to the jail swung open, drawing their attention. Gabe walked inside, followed by Noah.

"Did you find the boys?" Shane stood, offering his chair to Noah, who waved him off.

"We did. They're at the clinic with the docs," Noah said. "They'll keep them until they're healthy enough to go back to the orphanage."

Removing his hat, Gabe set it on a hook by the door. "Both were cold and hungry. Jackson said Teddy was thin as a stick. Charlie told us the men hardly ever fed them. The men ate the food themselves. I just don't understand men like Hammer, Doubt, and the twins. Are they in the cells?"

"They are, and won't keep their mouths shut." Hawke pulled the keys from a desk drawer. "Do you want to see them?"

"I wouldn't mind never seeing them again." Gabe scrubbed both hands over his face. "Less than two weeks from Christmas and we have to deal with people like them."

Noah leaned against a wall, crossing his arms. "When's the circuit judge coming back, Gabe?"

"Not until after Christmas. A few weeks afterward."

"We could take them to Big Pine." Hawke looked around the corner to the cells. "It would sure quiet this place a good bit if they were gone."

Gabe stood, grabbing a hat from its hook. "I'll send a telegram to Sheriff Sterling. He'll know the judge's schedule. We'll need a buckboard and six deputies to get them to Big Pine. With weather coming in, could be two days over and two back."

"All's been quiet here, Gabe. I'll go with five other deputies," Hawke said. "You don't need to leave town for four days. Not with all the Christmas festivities the town has planned."

Gabe stopped by the door. "What festivities?"

"You don't know?"

"Know what?"

Hawke looked at Noah, then back at Gabe. "Well, your wife, Noah's, mine, and several other women have some activities planned leading up to Christmas Eve."

Gabe's jaw tightened. "Exactly what?"

Hawke massaged the back of his neck. "Well, there's a carnival inside the community building on Saturday. The local band is playing Sunday afternoon at the church. There's also a sale of baked goods to raise money for the orphanage, but I don't recall what day. There's—" Hawke stopped when Gabe held up his hand.

"I'll talk to Lena. I'm certain you're right about my wife having a hand in all of these festivities."

"It's always the same, boss." Hawke grimaced. "The fact is, all our wives are involved in most activities in Splendor."

"Hey, out there. When are we gonna get our food?"

The men shook their heads, not one of them moving toward the cells.

Chapter Thirteen

"It's time I ride back to town, Martha. Dante's been staying with Lena for several days. I need to get the boy home."

"I'm sure he's anxious to see you." She fiddled with the edge of her sleeve, not meeting his gaze. The mention of Dante brought back the sense of abandonment she'd felt when Cole returned to Splendor, no longer showing an interest in her.

"Thank you for all you've done. Please thank Gabe again. It will be nice to get back to our regular routine."

"Sure." He stared at the ground, not moving for several long seconds before clearing his throat. "I've made some terrible mistakes with you, Martha, and I am truly sorry. Do you think we could start over?"

She worried her lower lip, seeming to consider his request. "Would you give me time to consider?"

"As much time as you need. Though, I do have a request."

A small smile tipped the corners of her mouth. "What is that?"

"Perhaps you'd be open to having supper with me now and then until you decide if you'll forgive me."

His sincere request changed the smile to one which stretched across her face. "I might be open to the occasional supper."

Fingering the brim of his hat, he nodded. "That sounds real good, Martha. Real good indeed."

Heading outside, he stepped into the saddle of his already cinched horse. Cole took another look at the orphanage, seeing a tall, elegant figure in the doorway. Lifting his hand, he felt a tug when she returned the gesture.

The ride back to Splendor was uneventful and somewhat boring compared to all the activity of the last few days. He thought of Charlie, Teddy, and the third boy, and all they'd been through at the hands of the four men. If it had been Dante...

The truth was, if it had been up to him, he didn't know if the four men would've arrived at Splendor alive.

Spotting the town in the distance, he put the last week behind him, concentrating on Christmas. This would be the first one he and Dante spent together. He wondered if the boy was missing out by living in a small frontier town instead of New York. By the time he reached the town limits, he'd convinced himself Dante had everything a boy needed in Splendor.

He made his way to Gabe and Lena's home, dismounting when the door flew open.

"Papa!" Dante rushed down the steps into his father's arms.

Cole didn't believe he'd ever felt so certain Dante belonged with him as he did at that moment. Tightening his hold for a moment, he loosened his arms.

"I missed you, Papa."

"I missed you, too. Are you ready to ride home?"

"Yes. I have to say goodbye to Miss Lena and Jackson. He told me you were at the orphanage."

"Both of us were there. Jackson did a good job of getting another boy to talk." Cole looked up to see Lena and Jackson on the porch. She held the hand of three-year-old Emma. He took the steps two at a time to stand in front of them. Removing his hat, he kissed Lena's cheek, nodded at Jackson, then smiled at Emma.

"Thank you for letting Dante stay here. Someday, I hope to repay you."

"Don't you know there's no need to repay me, Cole? This is what we do for friends."

"Well, I appreciate what you did."

"Sometime soon, we'll have you and Dante over for supper."

"I'm not going to turn down a meal from you, Lena. Guess I'd better get Dante home."

"Be safe, Cole."

Martha watched through the window of her small home in Splendor, sipping a cup of hot tea. Since arriving home the previous evening, a new storm had blanketed the town with over two feet of snow.

Cole and Dante had visited earlier that morning with two shovels. A normal one that Cole used, and one with a short handle Noah had built for Dante. The duo had shoveled snow from her steps and porch, then proceeded to clear a large area on the street outside her home. She'd rewarded them with hot chocolate and cookies.

School had been postponed again, leaving the town children with little to do. When she learned Dante would be spending the day at the jail, she'd volunteered to keep him with her. Though reluctant to take advantage, Dante's pleas to stay had won.

Glancing over her shoulder, warmth spread through her at the sight of Dante sleeping on her sofa. "Such a sweet boy," she whispered to no one. Swallowing the lump lodged in her throat, she turned back to the scene outside.

The storm hadn't lessened in intensity as she'd hoped. She estimated another foot of snow had fallen since Cole left for the jail. When Dante woke up, they'd walk the short distance to the meat market, where she'd buy a chicken, vegetables, and bread made each day by the owner's wife. And if they were lucky, there'd be a dried apple pie left in the glass display case. Cole's favorite, if her memory was accurate.

"Miss Martha?"

She hadn't heard him wake up and cross the room. "How was your nap?"

"Fine." His eyes grew wide at the amount of snow falling. "May I go outside, Miss Martha?"

"We both can. I need some items from the market. You are the perfect young man to help me."

"The one with the chickens?"

"Yes." She slipped into her coat, handing Dante his.

"Papa and I go there almost every day. He likes their pie."

Chuckling, she handed mittens and the matching knit cap Cole's sister had sent from New York. "If the market still has any, we'll bring one home for supper."

His voice rose with enthusiasm. "Are we eating here?"

"If you and Cole want to."

"We do!"

Laughing, she opened the door and shivered as she stepped down to the street. "This is going to be a quick trip, Dante."

Joining her, he lifted his face to the falling snow. Opening his mouth, he tried to catch flakes with his tongue. Laughing with each attempt, he continued as she watched. She'd been surprised to learn one of her favorite pastimes was watching the children play. Inside or outside, it didn't matter. She loved how they gave themselves completely to whatever activity Amy and Rose planned.

"Are you ready, Dante?"

"One more time." Stepping to the center of the street, he spread out his arms, and again opened his mouth.

It was then Martha spotted the buckboard, pulled with two large horses, head straight for them.

Martha's hand shook too much to catch all of the tears streaming down her cheeks. She had a fleeting thought of how her mother would be embarrassed by her show of emotion in public.

"I screamed, waved my arms," she sputtered to no one as she was the only person in the clinic waiting room. Her mother would be mortified at her daughter's behavior.

Doctor Ralston had treated her leg and arm while Doctor McCord started on Dante. Her injuries were painful but not critical. Dante, though. Her chest heaved when she thought of the young boy who'd trusted her.

Georgina Wise, a clinic nurse, had come out once to check on her before patting her shoulder and returning to help Doctor McCord. She'd learned nothing of Dante's condition from Georgie. There'd been a scant few seconds to dry her eyes and straighten her posture before Georgie got a good look at her. An image of her mother's perfection rolled across her mind before she ruthlessly shoved it away.

The front door burst open, slamming the wall behind it. Cole rushed inside, along with fellow deputy Dutch McFarlin.

Standing, she stood erect, trying to portray a calm she didn't feel. It didn't work. He gently gripped her shoulders while looking her over.

"Are you all right, Martha? Are you hurt?"

She shook her head. "Fine. I'm, uh...fine. It's Dante. He..." Unable to contain a sob, tears began streaming down her face.

He took the handkerchief from her, using it to dab at her face. "What has the doctor told you?"

"Nothing. Georgie came out once, but went straight back into the room."

"Dutch, will you stay here with Martha while I check on Dante?"

"Sure, Cole. That's why I'm here."

Squeezing her hand, he let out a long breath before knocking on the exam room door.

Cole had kept his emotions under control while talking with Martha. Inside, he shook with fear and anger. A great deal of fear about what he might learn on the other side of the door. A smaller amount of anger at Martha for not keeping his son safe.

Georgie opened the door. "Cole. We're not quite done in here."

Pushing past her, he walked to the bed, his stomach in knots. Dante lay on his back, his eyes closed. "How is he, Doc?"

"You shouldn't really be in here until we're done. But I understand. Right now, he's sleeping, not unconscious. Dante is a very lucky boy. He has a very nasty bump on his head, a sprained ankle, and a number of bruises. He also has come scratches on his face."

Cole lifted a hand to touch his son's face, then lowered it. "No broken bones?"

"No, which is amazing, given the driver of the buckboard never saw them. If it wasn't for Miss van Plew, it could've been much worse."

"What do you mean?"

The doctor looked toward the door, then back at Cole. "She ran in front of the buckboard to shove him out of the way. It didn't go how she'd planned. The wagon caught both of them, though her injuries aren't as bad. Dante could've been killed if she hadn't acted. Doc Ralston patched her up."

Cole let the doctor's words settle. Why hadn't Martha said anything to him? She'd tried to save Dante while putting herself in danger. And he'd been angry at her inability to keep him safe.

"When will he be ready to go home?"

"Give us another thirty minutes. I want to check him over once more to make certain nothing was missed."

Looking at Dante's sleeping face, he felt his heart squeeze. "I'll be out front with Martha."

"Georgie or I will be out to get you in a bit."

Feeling awful about how he'd assumed the worst about her, he opened the door and slipped out to the waiting area. His gaze scanned the room. Neither Martha nor Dutch were there.

The front door opened, and Dutch stepped inside, shaking off the snow. "It is darn cold out there."

"Where's Martha?"

"She asked if I'd walk her home. Did you know she was injured?"

"Doc McCord just told me." He shook his head. "She didn't say a word."

"Doesn't surprise me. I had to cajole it out of her. Anyway, she's at home. Resting, I'd guess."

Cole buttoned up his coat. "I'm going to check on her while they're finishing with Dante."

"How is the boy?"

"He'll be fine. He's real lucky."

"And fortunate Martha was with him."

"Yeah." Gripping the knob of the front door, he stopped when Georgie called to him.

"Cole. Dante's awake and asking for you. In fact, we had to hold him down before he jumped off the bed."

He hesitated a moment before going to his son, telling himself Martha needed rest. Tomorrow would be soon enough to thank her for all she'd done.

Chapter Fourteen

Redemption's Edge Ranch

"We're so glad Spencer brought you here, Dorinda. I can only imagine how difficult it was to live in the same home with your husband's second wife." Ginny Pelletier, Luke Pelletier's wife, sat with several other women at the dining room table as they constructed a Christmas quilt. "I'd have left the day he married her."

Dorinda offered a grim nod, already tired of discussing the events that prompted her to leave. "It was not an easy decision. The farm was my home."

"I hope you understand the ranch is now your home, for as long as you want to stay." Rachel Pelletier, Dax Pelletier's wife, hated the look of distress on Dorinda's face.

"It's a concept I don't understand." Lydia Mason, Bull's wife, finished a particularly difficult square before clipping the thread and setting down the needle.

"Multiple wives?" Ginny looked at Lydia.

"Yes." She shifted her attention to Dorinda, whose head was bowed over her work. "I know little about your faith, though it is intriguing."

Since arriving at the ranch, she'd said little about her faith. Less about how men were encouraged to take more than one wife. She knew her decision to leave was right, even if the deep pain of her husband's betrayal remained.

"Plural marriage is a doctrine of the Mormon faith." Dorinda licked her lips to hide her discomfort. "It is quite common, even though some husbands resist the pressure from our church leaders."

"Your husband didn't resist?" Lydia twisted the thimble on her finger.

"Yes, for a time. Jared made a promise to me before we married that he would never take a second wife." Dorinda let out a shaky breath. "I believed him."

The women grew silent as they concentrated on the quilt. Several minutes passed before Rachel spoke.

"As Ginny said, we're glad you're here with us. Joel is delightful."

This brought a smile to Dorinda's face. "He is a handful."

Rachel reached behind her to pick up her coffee cup, taking a sip. "Dax says Joel is a good listener. He gets along well with everyone, even the more crotchety ranch hands."

"Joel loves being around the men. He used to follow his father everywhere." Dorinda winced on the last, sorry she'd mentioned Jared. She didn't expect to hear from him again, and doubted he'd try to find her. He'd known of her pain at his decision to break his promise. Once the marriage to Clara was done, there was no returning to the life they'd once shared.

"Joel cannot wait to attend your school," Dorinda said.

"When Bull returned from the orphanage, he said school might not start up again until after Christmas." Lydia continued stitching.

"That's probably for the best," Rachel said. "I'm hopeful a new teacher for the town will be hired soon. The children here at the ranch attend school in town most days. When we have snow, such as now, they stay here, and all of us take turns giving them lessons. We all hope the town will hire someone soon."

Dorinda's head lifted from her work, her gaze on Rachel. "The town is seeking a new teacher?"

"Yes. Rose Keenan was the town's teacher, but she left to work at the orphanage. The town and rancher's children have been going there since school started again, but it's not the best solution. Even Martha van Plew, the administrator at the orphanage, has been helping with the search. Are you interested?"

The other women shifted to stare at Dorinda. All of them had children who attended school in town, or at the ranch during heavy snowstorms.

"I am not sure I am qualified."

"Many women are more qualified than they believe," Ginny said. "I'm not well educated, but I take my turn teaching when the weather is bad."

"It's the same with most of us," Lydia added. "Even Shining Star helps, even though she's still learning English."

Shining Star Zales, the wife of longtime ranch resident Billy Zales, had yet to speak. Their child was still too young for school, yet she'd helped several times when the weather worsened.

"Rose Keenan has offered her lesson plans to the new teacher," Ginny said. "If you can read, write, and know numbers, you have the knowledge to teach."

Dorinda clasped her hands together, setting them on the table. "It might be something I could do."

"Then we should talk to Martha van Plew and Ruth Paige," Rachel said.

"I met Miss van Plew at the orphanage when the stage stopped because of the snowstorm. She is very nice."

"Very nice...and smart." Rachel tapped her fingers on her section of the quilt. "When the weather clears, we'll ride into town and have lunch with Martha and Ruth. Ruth is Reverend Paige's wife."

Dorinda's initial excitement wavered. "A preacher?"

"Yes. Why?"

"They may not like I am of the Mormon faith. Or that I left my husband."

"I can't speak for Martha or the Reverend and Mrs. Paige, but I'm not sure those would be a problem. Perhaps if you were teaching Sunday school. The only way to know is to ask them. Unless you don't plan to stay in Splendor."

Dorinda startled at the comment. "My son and I will stay near Spencer. We are the only family he has left. We have nowhere else to go."

Cole gritted his teeth. He'd been listening to their four prisoners argue among themselves for hours, and was ready to toss buckets of water on each of them. If it weren't for Dante drawing figures of horses and people on some newsprint Cole had obtained, he would've done it.

He thought of Martha, wondering if she needed anything. Cole had stopped by her place the last two mornings to check on her. She'd refused to open the door both times.

When he and Dante left for lunch at the boardinghouse, they'd stopped at the clinic to see if Georgie had checked on Martha. Even if the nurse had gone by, Cole planned to buy extra food at the meat market and make a pot of stew for her.

"Do we get to visit Miss van Plew today, Papa?" Dante had paused in his drawing, his soulful green eyes searching Cole's.

"How about we make stew and take it to her?"

"She'd like that. Maybe biscuits, too."

"Great idea."

Dante sucked on his lower lip as if trying to solve a major problem. "Maybe I should take her the stew. She might open the door for me."

It often amazed him what his eight-year-old son said. "I'll go with you, but you can knock on the door."

"You have to stay back a few feet, Papa. She might not open the door if you're next to me." His serious expression pressed against Cole's heart.

"You're probably right."

Setting his pencil down, Dante covered his ears at another argument between the prisoners. Cole chuckled at the image he made.

"Why do they always yell, Papa?"

"I guess they don't know any other way to talk."

"You should teach them. Or maybe Miss van Plew can come and teach them when she's better."

Cole winced at the thought of trying to teach Doubt and his gang anything. He also knew there wasn't a chance Martha would offer her services.

Gabe had sent a telegram to the sheriff in Big Pine, but had yet to hear back. If Sheriff Parker gave his okay, they'd transfer the prisoners the minute the storm broke. The four would face a tough judge, which is what he and most others wanted.

Judge Collins, with his deep, robust, raspy voice, cut an interesting figure. His rotund frame, intimidating height, and stern demeanor usually stopped antics by the prisoners and their attorneys.

"I want to give this one to Miss van Plew for Christmas." He held up a drawing of a tall woman with several children around her.

The change of subject surprised Cole. Though it shouldn't. Dante had a habit of shifting his thoughts between subjects at a rapid pace.

"I'm sure she'd like the drawing, son."

"Maybe she'll put it up on a wall."

"She very well might do that."

"I have one for you, too. But you can't see it yet." Lowering his head, Dante worked on another drawing.

A cold wind swept through the jail when Gabe entered with longtime deputies Hex and Zeke Boudreaux. He waved a piece of paper in his hand.

"Sheriff Sterling finally sent a response to my request. Judge Collins says to get them to Big Pine quick, as he won't be holding trial after December twenty-third."

Cole took the telegram from Gabe's outstretched hand. Reading it, he handed it back. "What about witnesses?"

"If the judge operates as he has in the past, he'll take written statements made in front of an attorney if at least two witnesses show up in court. My thoughts are to have Teddy, Charlie, Joey, Bull, and Noah provide written statements. I'll ride over with you and Martha."

"Martha?" Cole shook his head. "Wouldn't it be better to have her write a statement?"

"Having a woman testifying in front of Judge Collins would help us out. She's formidable, smart, and will present a strong case against the four kidnappers."

"What about Rose or Amy?"

"They won't be quite as good. But if Martha refuses to go, I'll talk to one or both of them."

"Maybe Rose and Amy would want to go just to see Big Pine. Both like to shop," Hex quipped from his position near the woodstove.

"He has a point," Cole said. "We'd have to get Doc McCord's approval for Martha to travel."

Gabe gave a slow nod. "I forgot about her accident." He touched Dante's shoulder. "How are you doing?"

"Good." He held up one of his pictures for Gabe to see. "This is Miss van Plew."

"Nice, partner." He beamed at Gabe's praise. "A written statement from Martha might be best. I'd like to take the prisoners over tomorrow. With the stage not coming through town right now, the witnesses should go with us. I sent a telegram to the judge asking how many people he needed from Splendor. If it's one or two, I'll testify, along with one of the deputies."

Cole relaxed a little. He figured Gabe would select Morgan, Jonas, and Tucker to guard the prisoners on the way to Big Pine. All had helped to arrest the four. Any or all would make good witnesses.

"Why don't you and Dante head home? We're fine here until I get a response from the judge."

Cole slipped on his coat, helped Dante with his, then rolled up the drawings inside the unused newsprint. "Let's get going, son."

Dante stopped at the door to look up at Cole. "Maybe Miss van Plew will let you talk to her this time."

Shaking his head, Cole ushered his son outside. As he closed the door, he could hear robust laughter.

Chapter Fifteen

Martha stared out the window and smiled. The storm had subsided overnight, leaving a sky showing patches of bright blue.

Watching the few flakes of snow float in the air, she sighed at the loud knocking on her front door. Rising from the table, where she'd been indulging in her third cup of tea, she opened the door an inch.

"Rachel. What a nice surprise. Come inside before you freeze."

"I hope we aren't disturbing anything." Rachel stepped inside, turning toward her companion. "Dorinda, you already know Miss Martha van Plew, the force behind our orphanage. Martha, I believe Dorinda would make a wonderful candidate for the open teacher position."

Martha smiled. "Well, that's wonderful. Sit down and I'll make us all a cup of tea."

"I heard you had an accident. Are you all right?" Rachel sat down, motioning for Dorinda to do the same.

"It's been several days, and yes, I'm doing quite well. I plan to return to the orphanage today for a few hours."

"You might want to reconsider. Some are predicting a new storm to come through that's worse. The temperature does seem to be dropping." Rachel took the two empty cups from Martha's hands, setting both next to the teapot as another knock sounded. "You're popular this morning."

Martha cast an uneasy look at Rachel as she opened the door. She expected to find Cole. "Dante. It's good to see you."

"My papa made this for you." He held out the pot. "Papa says you can warm it up."

Taking the pot, she smiled. "Cole didn't need to do this."

"He wanted to. We both did." His broad smile was quick and sincere.

"Please thank him for me."

"I will!" He whirled away from her. Taking the steps to the street, he disappeared around the corner of her house.

Martha set the pot on the stove to start warming, then took a seat at the table. "From Cole and Dante Santori. Do you know them, Rachel?"

"I do. Cole introduced us to his son after church a few weeks ago. I didn't know he'd been married."

"He hasn't. At least, I don't recall him saying as much." Martha shrugged, lifting her cup for a sip of tea.

She needed to change the subject. "So, Mrs. Heaton, you're interested in the teaching position. I will say upfront that I do not make the decision on who to hire. There is a committee that interviews interested candidates and makes a decision. Since I'm a member of the committee, I can recommend an interview. Since we have children from five to eighteen years of age, it's imperative the teacher be able to provide lessons at different grade levels. We do have a schoolhouse, and the town is quite generous in providing funds for books and supplies. Are you still interested?"

"Yes. If I am qualified." She glanced at Rachel, who nodded. "I should let you know that I am of the Mormon faith, and have left my husband. He still lives on our farm in Utah, near Salt Lake City."

"I see. Well..." Martha inhaled, exhaling slowly. "Our teachers focus on reading, writing, and numbers, plus history and geography. The older children have lessons in science at a rudimentary level. There are also discussions on integrity and morality. Quite often these lessons include Bible verses and examples using people from the Bible. Not the Book of Mormon, Mrs. Heaton. Are you familiar with the Christian Bible?"

"Yes. We attended the Christian church until I was thirteen. That was when my parents made the decision to convert to the Mormon faith."

"Are your intentions to leave the Mormon faith?"

Dorinda thought about the question for a moment, before shaking her head. "I have made no decision."

"Would it offend you to use relevant verses and people from the Christian Bible?"

"We are taught the two books support each other."

"All right. About your husband. Is he a violent man? For instance, might he arrive at the school with the intent of hurting you, or taking you back to Utah by force?"

"No. Jared Heaton is a peaceful, quiet man. He would never hurt me or any child."

"Good. Now tell me about your education and teaching experience."

"I am an excellent reader. My cursive writing and grammar are quite good, as is my knowledge of numbers. I have a good grasp of history and geography."

"And science?"

"If the lessons are about basic concepts, such as plants and animals."

Martha filled each cup with more tea, taking a small sip of hers. "Tell me more about your experience."

Dorinda cast another glance at Rachel, who again nodded. "I am afraid I have no direct experience as a teacher in a schoolroom. I have helped our teachers, but that is all."

A small smile tilted one corner of Martha's mouth. "Do you believe you can teach our children?"

Heart pounding, she looked at the clasped hands in her lap, then raised her gaze to Martha. "Yes. I believe I would be an excellent teacher."

Martha nodded while sipping more tea. She looked at her friend, Rachel, whose expression remained neutral. She returned her attention to Dorinda.

"I believe you have a great deal to offer the children of Splendor. It would be my pleasure to encourage the committee to schedule an interview with you as soon as possible."

Martha abandoned her plan to visit the orphanage the instant she closed the door behind Rachel and Dorinda. Dark clouds had appeared while they'd talked over tea.

With her plans changed, she grabbed the book she'd been reading from her bedroom, setting it beside an overstuffed chair. The stew had warmed during the visit, the aroma drawing her toward the cast iron pot.

A good hour remained before the normal time for her to eat lunch. Too long in her estimation. Taking down a bowl from the cupboard, she placed two ladles of stew inside. She picked up a spoon and lowered herself into the comfortable chair.

The story captured her attention, as did the wonderful stew. Finishing, she set the bowl aside and closed her eyes.

Sometime later, she awoke to someone rapping on the front door. Shaking her head to wake up, she placed the forgotten book on the table and opened the door. Her mouth went dry.

"Cole."

"Hello, Martha. Do you have a few minutes?"

"Um...I suppose." She ushered him to the sofa. "Would you care for tea?"

"Nothing for me. Please feel free to make some for yourself."

She picked up the bowl, walking past him to the kitchen. "I believe I've had my fill. How about some of the wonderful stew Dante brought over?"

Chuckling, he shook his head. "I have some waiting at my place."

"The stew really is quite good." She watched him as she sat down. "Thank you. It was thoughtful of you."

The room grew silent for several beats before Cole spoke. "When I returned to the waiting room, you were gone."

"Yes. I'm sorry for abandoning you. Exhaustion claimed me, and I had to get home."

"That's not quite true." He smiled.

"What?"

"Your injuries were also hurting, right? Injuries from saving Dante." He saw color creep up her face.

"They are minor."

"Doc McCord said they were less than Dante's, but not minor."

"I see."

"How are you feeling?"

"I'm not sure it's any of your business, Cole."

"You were protecting my son, Martha. That makes it my business." He leaned toward her. "Tell me how you're doing. Please."

She pursed her lips, then nodded, more to convince herself than for Cole. "I'm healing well. The bruises are fading."

"Are you still in pain?"

"There's no pain. The injuries were more annoying than painful. Is that all?"

"Do you have any coffee?"

The change of subject startled her. "I can make some."

"I'd appreciate it. The storm is getting worse. It'd be nice to warm up before going outside." In truth, Cole wasn't ready to leave. After staying at the orphanage for a couple days, he missed being around her. "I'll help."

"No, thank you." She rose. "The kitchen is a little small for two people. If you'd like, you can sit at the table."

Cole selected a chair closest to the kitchen, getting a better view of her actions. He didn't see her wince in pain, or favor one leg over another. When she raised an arm to remove coffee grinds from the cupboard, she made no indication it bothered her. All good signs.

"When will you be returning to the orphanage?"

"I'd planned to go today. The storm stopped me. Perhaps tomorrow."

Martha moved with an elegant grace, the same as always. She set the pot on the stove. Instead of sitting down at the table, she leaned against the counter.

"Where is Dante today?"

"Gabe brought Jackson with him to the jail. The boys were playing checkers when I left."

"I understand from Lena that Jackson is quite good at chess. Perhaps he'll teach Dante." She glanced out the kitchen window. "This is certainly the day for it."

A knock drew their attention. She chuckled as she walked past Cole to the door. "I can't recall a day I've had so many visitors."

Opening it a crack, she opened the door. "Sheriff Evans. What a nice surprise. Please, come in. Are you here to see me or Cole?"

Removing his hat, he held it by his side. "Both of you."

"Sit down and I'll get you some coffee."

"None for me, Martha. I have to get back to the jail." Gabe looked at Cole. "I received a telegram from Sheriff Sterling. He spoke with Judge Collins. The judge agreed to allow me and the deputies who'll be taking the prisoners to Big Pine to testify in person. He'll accept written testimony from four others who witnessed the event. The trial has already been scheduled, so we have to obtain the written statements right away." He looked back at Martha. "We'll need your statement. Frannie Boudreaux is available for us. Two of my deputies will ride to the orphanage as soon as there's a break in the weather to take statements from Amy and Rose."

Martha looked between Gabe and Cole. "When do you want to do this, Sheriff?"

Gabe settled his hat back on his head. "Right now."

Chapter Sixteen

"All right, ladies. There are eight days left before Christmas. We have a lot of work ahead of us." Ruth Paige stood in front of a group of women in the community building. "We're lucky the storm moved on. If the luck continues, it will remain clear until after Christmas. Everyone has volunteered for specific jobs. Let's start with decorations for this building. Are there any questions?"

Martha looked at the women around her. Angela Banderas, her close friend since their time together in New York, sat next to her. Friends she'd made since arriving in Splendor surrounded them. All looked toward Ruth with expectant gazes.

Many had been through Christmas preparations before and were anxious to get to work. Angela leaned toward her, whispering close to her ear.

"Are you decorating the orphanage?"

Martha sighed. "Yes. I plan to ride there later tomorrow and spend the night."

"Does anyone else have questions?" Ruth scanned the group. "If not, let's get started."

"Are you riding alone?"

"The same as I always do."

"Someone should ride with you, Martha."

"Besides not needing an escort, there's no one with the time. I can't think of anyone who isn't busy with Christmas preparations."

A knowing smile appeared on Angela's face. "What about Cole?"

"He has Dante."

"I'm sure Dante would be excited about staying overnight at the orphanage."

Martha's brows drew together. "How would you know?"

"Shane was in the jail when the storm was at its worst. Dante was there with Jackson. Both boys told him they'd like to go out there before Christmas to see their friends."

"Interesting. I hadn't considered they might want to wish the children a Merry Christmas."

"They may even want to take presents." Angela pulled a roll of bright red ribbon from one of the storage crates.

"Dante can't afford presents."

"Jackson might even talk Lena and Gabe into something from both boys. After all, they don't have to be extravagant." Angela cut several lengths of ribbon, handing them to Martha.

"Few presents are."

Their conversation came to a halt when several women joined them around the ribbon crate. Martha couldn't put it out of her mind. Not the rest of the day or the following until well after lunch.

Finishing the last of the stew, she packed a small satchel before rallying her courage to find Cole. He hadn't returned since visiting the same day the storm started. She hadn't decided how to phrase her request without embarrassing herself. Asking for donations or help never bothered her. Except when asking Cole.

Slipping into her heavy coat, she left the satchel by the front door before walking to the jail. All the way, she practiced her request. Just before opening the jail door, she sent up a prayer for Cole to listen with an open mind.

Cole slapped the lines of the wagon, his smile growing as he thought of the day before. Glancing at Martha, who sat next to him, he couldn't hold back his thoughts.

"Did you really think Gabe or I would turn you down?" He didn't miss the flush which crept into her cheeks. Even considering the cold, he knew his question surprised her.

"Honestly, I had no idea what either of you would say. I don't know either one of you well enough to guess."

"You know me, Martha. Better than anyone in Splendor."

She shifted to look at him. "At one time, I would've agreed with you. When you left for New York, without any real explanation, then returned with Dante and didn't seek me out, I accepted I didn't know you at all."

Cole's jaw twitched, though he remained silent. Slapping the lines to keep the horses moving through the snow, he glanced around. More to give himself a moment to think than to search for danger.

He heard Dante and Jackson talking in the back of the wagon. They'd huddled between two crates containing ribbon and other items to decorate the orphanage for Christmas. Around them were packages of bread, dried fruit, and meat.

The back of the wagon held two more crates filled with presents for the children. Many were obtained from the Splendor Emporium. Owners Josie Lucero and Olivia McCord donated most of the items they'd purchased from local men and women who worked on them throughout the year.

One crate held simple items such as dolls, carved animals, and games. On top were packed mittens, scarves, and socks. The other contained candies, cookies, and sweet breads. Rare luxuries the children were seldom given.

Cole glanced at Martha, noting the way her lips pinched at the corners. She'd expected a response to her voiced thoughts instead of his long silence.

"When I left Splendor, I didn't know how long the trip would last. My oldest sister, Camilla, had sent me a letter with a plea to return home. She didn't say why, but I knew the letter couldn't be ignored. My family is, well...rather well-off. I am the youngest of eight children. My father was quite ill. Camilla sought to put old grudges aside before it was too late."

Martha met his gaze. "Old grudges?"

"My father was never a temperate man. Growing up in his home carried little joy and many harsh reprimands. A good deal of them were the result of my mother's high standards. She set the rules. When broken, my father doled out the punishment." Cole gave a slight shake of his head as if casting off the bad memories.

"There were three reasons Camilla sent for me. The first had to do with making peace with my father and mother. The second, I'd suspected for a long time." He grew silent for a moment before letting out a tired breath. "My mother's last pregnancy resulted in a miscarriage. Afterward, she'd settled into a deep depression. Father couldn't handle her sadness, so he decided to fix what he saw as an unbearable situation."

Martha remained silent, her gloved hands clasped in her lap. "Yes?"

"Father visited the hospital, returning home with a newborn baby boy of Italian descent."

"Oh, my..." Martha's voice trailed off.

"They named him Columbus Marco Dante Santori."

"Cole Santori," she whispered.

"Yes."

The wagon continued to move along without him noticing, his thoughts on a small boy who'd never quite fit into the strict and formal world of the Santori family.

"That is...I mean, well...such an incredible story."

He looked at her, his features softening. "Yes, it is." Swallowing the odd lump in his throat, he continued. "When I was sixteen, my parents sent me away to school. I didn't want to be there, so I ran away."

"And you never returned home until receiving your sister's letter."

"How did you know?"

"A guess." She offered him one of her brilliant smiles. "So, that was the second reason she wanted you to return. What is the third?"

"The third is the boy talking with Jackson in the back of the wagon."

"I suspected as much. Tell me the rest."

Cole glanced over his shoulder to confirm Dante wasn't listening. "His mother, Evelyn Anderson, was a young widow when we met in Kansas City. She was the sweetest woman I'd ever met, as was her two-year-old son, Dante. I fell hard. I offered marriage, but her family had other plans. Before she left to return east, I promised to take care of Dante if anything ever happened to her."

"Oh, no. So this means..."

"Evelyn and her parents died in a tragic accident." He explained how Evelyn's good friend knew of his offer to take Dante. Camilla had accepted him into her home before sending the telegram to Cole. "At first, I wasn't sure he should be moved from a life he knew."

"And now?"

"I can't imagine life without him."

Reaching over, she placed a hand on his arm. "You're a good man, Columbus Santori."

"A good man wouldn't have let fear keep him from talking to you earlier about all this, Martha. I hope there's a chance to make up for the time we lost."

"I do believe we can work something out." An impish grin curled the corners of her mouth.

The children at the orphanage were more than a little excited when the wagon stopped by the front steps. Dante and Jackson jumped out, running to meet the boys and girls as they rushed toward them.

Cole marveled at how Martha organized the children into age groups to help unload the wagon. When everything sat in the living room, she and Cole opened the crate filled with decorations.

The younger children were tasked with attaching pine boughs to the railings leading upstairs, and outside on the porch. The older children made bows out of the red ribbon. Amy and Rose supervised, leaving Martha and Cole to move the presents into a store room, which he believed had once been a study.

When those activities were complete, everyone headed outside to find the perfect Christmas tree. The number of children had swelled over the months to fourteen, including Joey, the boy who'd been held captive with Teddy.

With so many opinions on what represented a perfect tree, it took an hour to find one and return it to the house. Hauling the tree up the steps and into the house took another fifteen minutes.

"Can we decorate it now?" A girl of about six, with bright red curls, jumped up and down, pointing to the tree.

"After lunch. Miss Amy is ready for us in the dining room." Martha ushered the children into a room that Noah and his men had enlarged to include what had once been a parlor. A twelve-foot table and mismatched chairs took up the entire space.

After saying grace, the children ate their potato with ham soup and every biscuit Amy had made. They laughed, talking excitedly about decorating the tree. Many mentioned how Christmas had been celebrated in their homes before losing their parents. Those who'd never had a family listened, with their eyes wide open and a brief look of longing on their faces.

Amy and Rose sat in the kitchen, resting at the table after several days of supervising the children. Martha and Cole took turns checking on the children and offering second helpings of soup. The older boys gladly accepted while the younger ones were too excited to eat much.

The children returned to the living room after everyone had eaten their fill. They sat on the floor, legs crossed, waiting for Martha's nod to decorate the tree.

Over the laughter, Cole almost missed someone pounding on the front door. He looked through a window to see a lone man standing on the porch, rubbing his hands together.

Hand on the butt of his six-shooter, he opened the door. The man had a weather-beaten face and red splotches from the cold. He wore a beard, and as Cole inspected him, he realized the stranger was younger than he'd first thought. The man didn't wear a gun or hold a weapon in either hand. When a burst of laughter came from behind

Cole, the man looked around him, a sad expression settling on his face.

"Are you looking for someone?"

The man straightened. "I have traveled a long way on my search."

Martha moved to stand next to Cole.

"Who are you searching for?" Cole asked.

He lifted his chin. "My wife."

Chapter Seventeen

Martha sucked in a breath. Her hands fisted at her sides as she took another good look at the man. He stood ramrod straight, his gaze locked on Cole. He wore a black coat, pants, and flat-crowned hat. His dark beard showed slight traces of gray, and rested on the outside of his coat.

"Who are you?" Martha saw a flicker of something in his eyes, then it was gone. He paid her no attention, focusing on Cole.

"I am Jared Heaton. My wife left the farm with our son. I have come to take them home."

"What is her name?" Martha tried again, seeing the same blank look in the man's eyes. He looked to Cole.

"My wife is Dorinda Heaton. Our son is Joel. Do you know them?"

Cole didn't answer. "Come inside. It's cold out, and the chill is entering the house."

Jared hesitated a moment, nodded, and stepped into the warm house. "Thank you."

The children stilled at the entrance of a strange man. Without a word, the younger ones began moving toward the older children. Jackson, Teddy, and two more of the older boys stood in front of the group.

"Children, this is Mr. Heaton. He is searching for someone." Martha looked at Amy and Rose, her voice calm and reassuring. "Please return to what you were doing."

"What is this place?"

Martha replied. "An orphanage, Mr. Heaton. We can talk in the kitchen without interruption."

"I will speak to your husband."

Cole stepped up to him. "I'm a deputy sheriff for Splendor, not her husband. And all three of us will talk about your reason for being here."

Jared stopped to look at Cole as if he were assessing his truthfulness. After a moment, he nodded. "All right."

"May I get you some warm milk to take away the chill, Mr. Heaton?"

"Yes. Thank you."

Cole motioned to the table and chairs. "Sit down and we'll talk. First, I am Cole Santori, and this is Miss Martha van Plew. She is the administrator of the orphanage."

She nodded to Jared from her spot by the stove.

"As I said, I'm a deputy sheriff. Tell us more about the woman you seek." Cole sat down across from Jared, thanking Martha for the cup of coffee she placed in front of him.

"Dorinda is a good woman with brown hair and eyes." He thanked Martha for the warm milk, staring into it as she sat down. "She is a loyal wife."

"And a good mother?" Cole asked.

Jared seemed to consider this. "Yes. We planned for more children, but were not blessed with them."

Cole looked at the man over the rim of his cup. "Do you believe she was kidnapped, or did she leave your farm voluntarily?"

Staring into the cup of warm milk, Jared took his time. "Is it important?"

"It makes a difference. If kidnapped, she wants to be found. If she left of her own free will, she doesn't. If she doesn't, there must be a reason behind her decision to leave."

Jared finished his milk, set the cup aside, and stood. "Is there a boardinghouse in town?"

"Yes," Cole answered. "You'll be entering from the south. The boardinghouse is at the north end of town on your left. If you reach the schoolhouse, you've gone too far."

"Thank you. I will leave you in peace."

Cole and Martha followed him to the door, standing on the porch until he climbed onto his buckboard and vanished around a curve in the road.

"Interesting." Martha returned to the warmth of the house, Cole right behind her.

"What part do you find interesting?"

They stood in the entry, watching the children decorate. Dante looked in their direction and waved. His joy showed in his eyes and on his face.

"Your question rattled Mr. Heaton. He doesn't want to admit his wife ran away."

Cole continued to watch the children. "He's asking about Dorinda Heaton."

"Yes."

"When I met her the night the stage stopped here, she didn't give the impression her brother was taking her to the Pelletier ranch against her will."

"She wasn't. Dorinda left the farm voluntarily. In fact, she has an interview with the committee searching for a town teacher."

"Does she have a chance?"

"I believe she does. Rachel Pelletier is her sponsor."

Cole's brows rose. "Impressive. You put her name to the committee?"

"Yes. There are a couple issues the committee must consider. If those can be worked out, I believe Dorinda would make a wonderful teacher."

"Will you be interviewing her with the others?"

"No. I've already made up my mind. But I will be in the room. So, what should be done about the arrival of her husband?"

"There's nothing we can do, Martha. It's a matter between the two of them."

"Can he force her to leave with him?"

"I don't believe so. I'm going to speak with Gabe when he returns from Big Pine. Do you have time to speak with Frannie Boudreaux?"

"I'll make the time. It will be the second time in a week I'll have spoken with her."

Cole had heard Martha's meeting with Frannie about what happened at the orphanage had gone well.

"Enough about the Heatons. I'd like to do something more uplifting. Care to help with the decorations, Deputy Santori?"

"Can't think of a reason not to, Miss van Plew." He reached over to take her hand in his and squeezed.

"Your own education is impressive, Mrs. Heaton." Lena Evans smiled, intending to lessen the tension in the room.

"Thank you, Mrs. Evans."

"The committee would like to discuss your application." Lena looked at the others in the room. "I believe we will have a decision by this afternoon."

Dorinda gave an almost imperceptible nod. "Thank you for the opportunity."

Gathering her heavy coat, she walked to the end of the room before slipping into it. The interview had been exhausting, though she felt good about her answers. She hadn't waivered, giving an honest response to each question. The two issues of concern couldn't be changed.

Stepping into the cold, she walked away from the St. James Hotel and across the street to McCall's. The busy restaurant had fewer tables than the boardinghouse, but served wonderful hot chocolate. It was also where Martha had asked her to wait while the committee made a decision.

The interview provided answers to several questions she had about the position. Dorinda now knew the salary, what they expected of her, and that the position came with a house in town. Though it had one bedroom, she believed Joel and she would be comfortable.

She took a table near the back, but facing the windows in the front. Betts Jones brought out a large cup filled with steaming hot chocolate within minutes of the order.

"If you want more, just holler." Betts left to greet an older couple.

She relaxed more with each sip. Dorinda wasn't certain what she'd do if they didn't offer her the teaching job. Rachel had assured her there was always plenty of work at the ranch. The knowledge comforted her. Either way, there would be a place to live, food, and many ways to contribute.

"Would you like another one, honey?" Betts waited by her table. An imposing woman, she stood about five-feet-eight, carried around one hundred and sixty pounds, and wore her gray-streaked brown hair in a tight bun.

"I should not have another, but..."

"One more cup of hot chocolate will be out in a minute." She swept the empty cup from the table, taking it with her to the kitchen.

Dorinda again thought of the interview. She didn't want to admit how much the teaching position meant to her. The job would make her truly independent for the first time in her life.

"Here you are." Betts set down the chocolate. "Would you like a slice of sweet bread?"

"Not right now, thank you."

"If you change your mind, let me know. I'm Betts. I don't believe I've ever seen you in here."

"This is my first time. I am supposed to meet Martha van Plew."

Betts smiled. "Martha is a real nice lady. What's your name?"

"Oh, sorry. My name is Dorinda."

"Pleasure, Dorinda. Enjoy your chocolate."

Pulling the large cup closer, she enjoyed the aroma of the chocolate. Lifting it, she brought it to her lips and froze.

Lowering the cup, she stared outside, confirming the man standing on the boardwalk was Jared Heaton. She lowered her head and slipped down in the seat, praying he wouldn't spot her.

Scared to raise her head, she sat motionless. The bell above the door jingled, an indication someone had entered the restaurant. Daring to take a peek, she relaxed when she saw Martha walking toward her.

"Are you all right, Dorinda?"

She straightened in her chair, gaze darting around Martha toward the door. He was gone.

"I, um, thought I saw my husband outside the restaurant."

"Ah." Martha sat down. "It may have been best to warn you."

"Warn me?"

"I didn't want his presence in town to make a difference in your interview."

"You knew about Jared being here?"

"He showed up at the orphanage yesterday. Cole and I talked to him, but said nothing about you. It was my decision not to tell you. I planned to do it now when I also had good news."

The pounding in her heart had begun to slow as Martha's words sank in. "You also have good news?"

"Yes. We want to offer you the teacher position."

Tears burned the back of her eyes before several painted a trail down her face. Swiping at them, she smiled. "That is good news. The best." She pulled a handkerchief from the pocket of her skirt, using it to dry her cheeks. "I do not know how to thank you."

"All I did was suggest you for an interview. The rest was up to you."

Betts set down a cup of hot chocolate in front of Martha. "Enjoy yourselves, ladies."

"Betts, wait. I want to introduce you to Splendor's new school teacher. This is Miss Dorinda Heaton."

"Congratulations, young lady. Would you care for another hot chocolate to celebrate?"

Dorinda put a hand over her stomach. "I am afraid not." She looked at Martha. "This one is my second cup."

"Holler if you change your mind."

The women sat quietly for several minutes before Martha broke the silence.

"I do apologize for not warning you about your husband."

"I understand. It was a wise decision. My stomach gave me no rest last night or this morning. Knowing Jared had followed me would have made it worse. What am I to do with him? Certainly, he will hear about me taking the position of teacher."

"You don't have to move into town right away. It may be best to stay at the ranch and let one of the ranch hands bring you and Joel to town each morning, and take you back when school is over. Though, the more I think about it, that isn't the real issue."

"Are you thinking Jared will come to the school?"

"What do you think, Dorinda?"

"Yes, I believe that is quite possible. I have shamed him by leaving. He will want to take me home to show we are not apart any longer."

"Do you want that?"

"No." She winced at how her voice carried within the small restaurant. "I will not go back. This is my life now. I am just afraid he will try to take Joel. It is his son he wants."

"If you believe it best, Joel could stay at the ranch until Jared gives up and returns to his farm. I'm certain Rachel will have no issue with him being there. Would he leave town with you and not take Joel?"

"Never. He wants his son. Jared no longer cares about me as anything more than a housekeeper and person to tend the garden." She hadn't voiced the thought until now. It brought a wave of intense pain in her chest. The boy she'd loved since they were fourteen was no longer hers.

"Let's think about this. It is doubtful he will be able to stay away from his farm for long. Correct?"

"Yes."

"Does the other woman know how to do the chores or work a farm?"

Dorinda's eyes lit in amusement. "I have never seen her do any work around the house. She knows nothing of farm chores."

"That means he doesn't have much time to find you before he must return. School doesn't start until a few days after Christmas. You will have preparations to make, but those can be done at the ranch. I see no need for you to come to town until school begins. Rachel will let everyone know to keep watch for Jared. It would be less stressful than moving to town right away."

"Yes, you are right."

"Excellent. Now you have a plan."

They were so busy talking, neither noticed a man approaching their table. By the time he stopped, it was too late.

"Hello, Dorinda. It is time to go back to the farm."

Her heart banged inside her chest. She wasn't prepared to speak with him. Thankfully, she didn't have to do anything.

Martha glanced around, realizing they were the only patrons still in the restaurant. "Mr. Heaton. Dorinda has no intention of leaving with you." She stood, her gaze locked on his. "She has made her decision, and I must tell you, there are a number of people who will prevent you from forcing her to leave. I suggest you return to your farm."

"I will not return without her and my son."

"I'm afraid your decisions have brought you to this place. Decisions which she had no part. Go back to your new wife and allow Dorinda to start over."

He looked down at his wife. "Dorinda?"

She forced herself to meet his gaze. "Miss van Plew is right. You broke your vow to me, betrayed my trust. It is time you returned to Clara."

"I still love you, Dorinda. My life with Clara is nothing when compared to what we had."

"You should have considered your vow to me before committing to a second wife. We talked about this many times before your marriage to Clara. You knew my feelings and chose to ignore them. I am sorry, but I no longer desire to be your wife."

"Is there nothing I can do to change your mind?"

"The only option is to divorce Clara, which I know you will not do." Dorinda shook her head. "So, no. There is nothing to do but let me go."

"Come, Dorinda. It's time to leave before there's little light."

Rising, Dorinda looked into eyes she'd loved most of her life. The pain almost buckled her knees. "Goodbye, Jared. I will pray for you."

Chapter Eighteen

Spencer was waiting for Dorinda at Martha's house, anxious to learn the outcome of her interview. He couldn't miss her red eyes when she came closer.

"What is it?"

"Jared found me."

"How could he know you would be here?"

She stepped closer. "Where else would I go, Spencer? You're the only family left. Jared knows you found work here, so..." Dorinda's voice broke on the last.

Opening his arms, she walked into them. "I won't let Jared take you and Joel away, Dorie. Neither will any of the men on the ranch. We'll let Sheriff Evans know. He'll speak to his deputies. You'll be safe here."

Moving out of his arms, she offered a tempered smile. "There is good news."

"Tell me."

"I have been offered the teaching position. A wage and house is provided by the town. I will start soon after Christmas."

"That's wonderful, Dorie."

"We will not move into the house until Jared has returned to his farm."

"I'll talk to Dax and Luke about taking you and Joel to the schoolhouse in the morning and picking you up when school is out."

"Thank you, Spencer."

"Where is Joel?"

"At the Evans' house, playing with Dante and Jackson."

They said their goodbyes to Martha and headed out.

"Do you know where Jared is staying?"

"Martha told me he asked about the boardinghouse."

Spencer nodded. "Does he have funds to stay here long?"

"I am not sure. His father is a church leader with a successful business. He may have given Jared money to find us."

"Then he could stay for a while."

"I do not believe so, Spencer. Clara knows nothing about running a farm or anything else. She does not cook, and never helped with housekeeping chores. I am sure he has someone feeding the animals. Still, he will have to return soon." She glanced at her brother. "I will pray for that."

Cole stood outside Martha's house that evening, his hand poised to knock. A wreath of pine cones and ribbons had been attached to the front door. He'd noticed wreaths and bows on several houses and businesses since returning to town from the orphanage.

An unwelcome sense of nervous unease had settled in his gut. This would be their first formal engagement since he and Dante returned from New York.

Releasing a deep breath, he rapped on the door three times and stepped back. He was about to knock again when it opened. Martha stood inside, looking radiant.

"Come in, Cole."

Once inside, he allowed his gaze to flow over her. "You look beautiful, Martha."

A blush appeared. "Thank you. I know it's ridiculous, I was a little nervous about tonight. You probably don't understand." She'd always been direct, which he appreciated.

"I do understand. It's not ridiculous at all."

"You feel the same?"

"Yes, I do. It's been much too long since we've had a supper engagement. All my fault."

"Well, that's good. At least we are starting from the same place. May I get you a cup of coffee before we leave?"

"I stopped by the Eagle's Nest and reserved a table." He chuckled. "May not be necessary, but Thomas said it was a wise idea."

"Thomas is such a gem. I understand he's been at the restaurant for a while." She slid her coat off a hook. Cole took it from her hand and helped her slip into it.

"According to Gabe, he was one of the first hires. I believe he was recently promoted to manager of the hotel and restaurant. A good choice. Are you ready?"

"I am."

Stepping outside, she slid her arm through his. The snow had been light for the last two days, giving the streets a beautiful glow.

"How was the interview with Dorinda?"

"She did quite well. Well enough we offered her the position."

"She accepted?"

"Of course." Martha chuckled. "She's thrilled at the wage and the house in town. There is the one issue." Their walk took them past the jail and onto the boardwalk of the main street.

"Her husband. Does she know he's here?"

"She does now." Martha explained how Jared had appeared at McCall's, and his conversation with Dorinda. "She held firm in her decision to stay in Splendor."

"Do you believe he'll try to take her back anyway?"

"Force her?"

"Yes."

"I don't know. Dorinda is concerned about him showing up at the school and creating a commotion. School won't start until several days after Christmas. Depending on the money Jared had, he may have to leave before then. She won't move into the house until after he leaves."

"Smart decision. I'll let Gabe know about Jared."

They crossed the street to enter the restaurant. "Look at all the decorations. It's so beautiful," Martha said as they approached the front desk.

Thomas seated them at a window table, the one Cole had requested. Thomas handed them the handwritten menu. "Save room for dessert."

They talked about the orphanage, the children, and Dante before the server set their plates in front of them. When halfway through, Cole set down his fork to look at her. He said nothing, just looked at Martha, a smile forming. It took her a moment to notice.

"What?"

"I'm wondering what took me so long to do this."

"Have supper?"

"Yes. And other things. I remember we used to pack a lunch and ride out of town to enjoy it. Do you remember Whisper Lake?"

"Of course. It's one of my favorite places." She took another bite of baked squab.

"Did you ride up there while I was gone?" He followed her lead and speared a piece of his elk steak.

"Yes. I never went alone, though."

"Is that right?"

"I wouldn't lie about a ride to the lake."

Picking up his wine glass, he took a sip, studying her face. "Who rode with you?"

"I'm not certain it's any of your business. However, it's no secret. Lena, Angela, and I rode there once."

Cole began to relax.

"Another time, Rachel and Ginny rode with me."

He grinned, relaxing even more.

"The third trip was with Doctor Ralston." Taking a sip of wine, a self-satisfied smile appeared.

"Doc Ralston, huh?"

"He's a very nice man, interesting, and quite handsome."

And single, Cole thought. "What are his intentions?"

Her brows drew together. "His intention was to ride with me to Whisper Lake."

He wanted to growl. "Is he courting you, Martha?"

She took a sip of her wine. Then another, drawing out the pleasure of seeing him squirm. "I don't believe he sees it as courting me, and neither do I. The ride was between two friends. Nothing more." She set her glass down, seeing his features relax. "Why?"

Thomas appeared, stalling Cole's response. "How were your meals?"

"Wonderful, as always, Thomas."

"Thank you, Miss van Plew. And yours, Deputy Santori?"

"Excellent. I believe we'll have dessert."

Thomas beamed. "We have a new dessert. It can only be offered during the winter, as it requires lots of ice."

"Why lots of ice?" Martha asked.

"Because it is made with ice cream. The chef calls it Baked Alaska."

"Baked Alaska! Oh, my. I heard about it before moving to Splendor. That's what I'll have."

"Deputy?"

"I'm afraid it would be you two against me if I don't. I'll have the same."

"Excellent. I'll let the chef know. It does take a little more time than our other desserts."

"I'm sure it will be worth it, Thomas." The excitement on Martha's face hit Cole in the chest.

"It will be."

After Thomas walked away, she touched Cole's arm. "This is going to be magical. I can't wait to try it."

"I'm certain you're right." He recalled other meals they'd shared. Martha ate with gusto, loving everything. The same as with anything she attempted. She'd jump right in and never complain.

"This wine is remarkable." She took another sip, holding the glass out to look at the dark red liquid.

"Tell me about the doctor."

"There isn't much to tell. Drake is easy to be around. We've become friends. We occasionally meet for breakfast." She shrugged as if it was inconsequential.

"I see." He didn't, but it seemed the correct response.

"Are you all right, Cole?"

"I'm fine. Tell me more about your relationship with Drake."

She glanced across the room, seeing the server approach. "Our desserts are here."

When the Baked Alaskas were in front of them, the meringue still flaming, the server excused himself. "Enjoy."

"This is incredible." Martha picked up a spoon, taking a bite. She saw he wasn't moving. "Cole, you have to try it before the ice cream melts."

Lifting his spoon, he took a mouthful, letting the ice cream melt in his mouth. The second bite was even better than the first.

"Well, what do you think?"

"It's good."

Several minutes later, she set down her spoon. "I can't eat another bite."

He continued eating until his plate was almost clean. "It was better than good."

"Yes, it was."

Taking a swallow of coffee, he placed the cup back on the table. "Tell me more about you and Drake."

"There isn't more to tell. We're friends. My best friend, Angela, is married. So is Drake's partner at the clinic. All we did was spend a little time together." She finished her tea, setting the cup down. "You seem upset, and I don't understand why."

"Because if Drake is courting you, I'll step aside."

She clasped her hands in her lap, tight enough so her knuckles turned white. "He's not, Cole."

"Are you sure?"

"Yes, I am quite sure. Drake is courting someone else. He has been since before you returned to Splendor. I should have made that clear to you when I first mentioned him."

Cole remained silent until he'd paid for their meal and escorted her outside. He dragged in a deep breath of ice cold air, and slipped her arm through his for the walk to her house.

"Are you sure you're all right, Cole?"

"Yes, I'm good. I shouldn't have assumed you and Drake were courting."

"My fault. I didn't explain very well," she said. "I'm not good at this."

"What?"

"Being courted. The truth is, until you, no man had shown an interest in me. Not seriously. A couple acted interested, but they were after a piece of my family's money. It's understandable."

They turned the corner at the jail. "What's understandable?"

"Well, I'm plain. Not pretty like Angela, or Carrie MacKenzie, or—"

"Stop, Martha."

"I'm trying to be honest."

"Well, you're wrong."

"I—"

Before she could finish, he stopped, turning her toward him. "Listen to me, Martha. You're the most beautiful woman I know. You're smart, funny, gracious. Everything a man could ever want." He looked away for an instant before meeting her gaze. "You're all I've ever wanted."

Before she could move or object, he leaned down and kissed her.

Chapter Nineteen

The kiss took her by surprise. Within seconds, she realized it was a good surprise. Quite good.

Her hands flattened on his chest, then moved to his shoulders. Within seconds, he pulled back, and it was over.

"I've wanted to kiss you for a while."

She waited for her heart to slow its rapid beating. "Oh?"

"Since the second time we went out to supper."

Cocking her head a little, a small smile appeared. "At the boardinghouse?"

"You remember?"

"I remember every time we met for breakfast, lunch, or supper. Plus the times we rode out of town."

"So do I." He slid her arm through his, continuing to her house. "Do you plan to attend Christmas Eve services?"

"Yes."

"Good. Then I'll escort you."

"I'd like to go with you and Dante, Cole. Very much."

They walked up the front steps of her house. "Would you care to come inside for coffee?"

"That would be nice." He stepped inside, helping her with her coat.

"I had a wonderful time tonight, Cole."

He walked to stand beside her. "So did I. Especially the Baked Alaska."

She laughed while setting the coffeepot on the cookstove. "Are you teasing me?"

"Not at all. I liked it. Doesn't mean I'll order it again."

This time, the laughter spilled from her. "I knew it. You'll order pie."

"How did you know?"

"Cole." Her mouth twisted into a sardonic grin. "You *always* order pie."

"You're the only person who's figured it out."

"Ask Dante. I'm sure he'll tell you the same." Lifting the pot, she filled two cups, handing one to him. She knew he didn't put anything in his coffee.

They sat down at the table, Martha fighting the urge to ask him her most pressing question. The one that had bothered her for months.

Cole watched the changing emotions on her face. "What are you thinking about?"

"Excuse me?"

He reached out, tapping her forehead. "You're pondering something in that beautiful head. Is there a question you're fighting hard not to ask me?"

Pursing her lips, she looked away for several seconds before returning her gaze to his. "Well, there is something."

"Ask me."

"Why have you waited so long to show you still have an interest in me?"

Rising, he walked to the cookstove to refill his cup. He stared out the window, took a sip of the hot liquid, and reclaimed his seat.

"I shouldn't have put off seeing you for so long."

"That's not an answer, Cole."

"I suppose not." He took another sip before leaning forward to rest his arms on the table. "Life became complicated during my trip to New York." He let out a breath. "Ending up with Dante was a surprise. I never thought my offer would happen."

"Offer?"

Cole gave her a slow nod. "I'll start at the beginning."

It took several minutes to relate how his relationship with Dante came about. He provided minimal information about his feelings for the boy's mother, Evelyn, or their departure from Kansas City. His proposal to raise Dante if anything ever happened to her sounded absurd in the retelling. Martha didn't interrupt as she absorbed the fascinating tale.

"You were single, had no job, and didn't know where you would go after Kansas City. Yet you offered to take a child you barely knew. It's more than a little curious." There was no censure in her voice.

"I suppose it is." He massaged the back of his neck. "Dante and I had an immediate bond. There is no other way it can be explained. I don't understand it myself."

"So when his mother and grandparents died, a friend of Evelyn's hunted down your sister, Camilla. It's amazing." Standing, she paced around the table, then back to her chair. Resting her hands on the back, she raised her head to the ceiling for a moment before continuing.

"Did you ever believe you would be approached to fulfill your quite generous offer?"

"Not once. My life continued, but I never forgot Evelyn or Dante. The trip to New York was a revelation in many ways. When we returned to Splendor, there were many explanations to be made. You should've been the first."

"Instead, I was the last." Sitting down, she rolled the coffee cup between the palms of her hands.

"Not because you weren't important. Other than Dante, you are the most important person in my life."

Her mirthless chuckle hung between them until Cole spoke again.

"This may not make sense, but I didn't want to disappoint you. I had no idea what you'd think of me having responsibility for a young boy. I was a coward, Martha. It was easier to avoid this discussion than risk you telling me we had no future."

She took his words in, rolling them around in her mind. "And now?"

"It was time to explain."

"And if I hadn't asked?"

"I would've explained. My plan was to talk with you before Christmas." When Martha didn't respond, he tapped his fingers on the table. "Do you have any more questions?"

"Not really. Well...maybe."

He stood, again filling his cup with coffee. Sitting back down, he leaned back in the chair.

"What are your intentions for us, Cole?"

"I want to keep seeing you."

"For how long this time? Do you believe there's a future for us?"

"My hope is we have a long future. You're the woman I want in my life."

"And in Dante's?"

"You would make a wonderful mother for him."

She was about to answer when a knock sounded on the front door. "Who would be visiting at this hour?"

Cole removed his pocket watch from his shirt. "It's eight o'clock, Martha." When she moved to stand, he stopped her with a hand on her arm. "I'll see who it is."

The knock came again, this time more insistent. Standing, he closed the distance to the door in several long strides. Opening it, he stared, his surprise genuine.

"Well, are you going to allow me in, Columbus, or make me stand in the cold?"

Opening the door wide, he wrapped his arms around the visitor. "What are you doing here?"

"It is such a pleasure to meet you, Camilla." Martha filled the cup in front of Cole's sister. "We were just speaking about Dante and your role in getting him to Cole. It's an incredible story."

"I suppose it is. It didn't seem so when Dante came into our lives." She looked at her brother. "Getting to Splendor was more difficult than expected."

"When did you arrive, and why did you wait so long at the hotel before locating me?" Cole watched his sister warm her hands around the hot cup.

"Hotel? I haven't found a place to stay since arriving less than an hour ago."

"An hour ago?"

"Yes, dear brother. It was a miracle we arrived at all."

His brows rose. "We? Was there a stagecoach this late?"

"Heavens, no. The stage broke down a mile east of Big Pine. A rare occurrence according to the station master. It took hours before anyone realized we might be in trouble and notified the sheriff. He and several deputies found us. By then, we were quite tired and anxious. After reaching town, on horseback, I might add, I had no intention of waiting until the repairs were made. It took time to locate the livery and negotiate transportation. On a buckboard!" A brittle laugh accompanied her comment.

Martha's eyes widened. "The trip must've been miserable."

"It was quite cold, especially after the sun disappeared. When it did, the driver stopped to retrieve a large hide, which he wrapped around me. Buffalo, I believe. Disgusting, but warm. Without it, I'm sure I would've perished from the cold." Picking up the cup, she drained the contents. "Do you have more?"

"Yes." Martha refilled the cup. "I'll make another pot."

"You are a dear."

"How did you find me?"

"The deputy at the jail was quite helpful, Columbus. He accompanied me to your house. When we realized you weren't there, he suggested coming here."

"I didn't see a deputy with you," Cole said.

"When we saw lights coming from Martha's house, I sent him on his way."

Rubbing his jaw, he shook his head. "You are remarkable, Camilla."

"Not true, but I was determined." She smiled before taking a sip of the coffee. "This is quite good. Better than we have at home. I had a cup at the jail. It tasted similar."

Martha lifted her canister. "When possible, many of us purchase coffee from the Eagle's Nest restaurant. The Evans family orders extra for locals."

"Oh, yes. I'd forgotten the connection with the Evans from New York. You are fortunate. I must find out where they procure this before returning home. Now, where is Dante?"

"He's staying with Lena and Gabe Evans."

"The same Evans?"

"Yes. Their son, Jackson, has befriended Dante. They share many of the same interests."

"How wonderful." Finishing the coffee, Camilla stood. "I must return to the jail to retrieve my bags. Then, I must locate lodging."

"I'll go with you." Cole stood, casting an apologetic glance at Martha. "We'll all have breakfast at the Eagle's Nest tomorrow morning. Will you join us?"

"I'd love to."

"Thank you for a wonderful evening, Martha."

"It was enlightening." She smiled, walking them to the door. "I'm so glad you chose to visit for Christmas, Camilla."

"As Columbus knows, our family is quite reserved. Christmas had always been, well, not as merry as in other households."

"We will have to change that for you." Martha opened the door to see a clear sky. "Christmas in Splendor is a true celebration. One you'll never forget."

Chapter Twenty

There were few tables available for breakfast at the Eagle's Nest the following morning. Cole knew most of the patrons, though there were several new faces. Given the stagecoach service had restarted their route two days earlier, the number of unfamiliar diners surprised him.

"There she is!" Dante pointed to a table near the back. "Miss van Plew is there, too." He started toward them, slowing when Cole reminded him to walk, not run through the restaurant.

"Aunt Camilla!" Dante gave her a hug.

"I do believe you've grown a foot since moving to Splendor. How do you like it here?"

"I like it." Turning, he greeted Martha. "Good morning, Miss van Plew."

"Good morning, Dante. Did you have fun with Jackson?"

He beamed at the question. "Yes. He taught me to play chess."

"Then I suppose you're an expert, and I should be careful when we play." Martha fought to keep a straight face.

Dante laughed. "Nooo. We can play after I beat Jackson." He took a seat next to her.

"I'll look forward to it."

Cole walked around the table, kissing both women on the cheek, then taking a chair across from Martha. "Hope we didn't keep you waiting."

"Not at all," Camilla answered. "I've been noticing the décor. I certainly didn't expect such a nice restaurant when I left New York. And my room is quite nice."

"If there's anything you need, Thomas is the manager." Cole showed Dante how to place the napkin on his lap.

"I know, Papa. Mama showed me."

Cole shot a look at the women. Both smiled back.

Dante held the menu in both hands, reading the food available.

"I want bacon and eggs, Papa."

"Good morning, ladies and Deputy Santori." Thomas bowed toward Dante. "Master Santori. May I take your orders?"

"Bacon and eggs." Dante grinned at Cole.

"Excellent choice."

A few minutes later, he'd written down orders for the adults. "I'll bring more coffee. And hot chocolate for you, Master Santori."

Dante giggled as Thomas walked away.

"Tell me what the people of Splendor are doing for Christmas."

Cole nodded at Martha to answer. "The children are putting on a play before Christmas Eve service. Dante is part of the performance."

Dante smiled at Camilla.

"The town choral is performing a concert tomorrow night and the following. I'll be singing with them. The church women are having baked goods sales on both nights. I heard the St. James Hotel is offering free hot cider and cookies. I don't know when. We can ask Thomas. Ruby's Palace is putting on a special Christmas show starting tomorrow night." She looked at Cole. "It's for children and adults. Ruby will also offer hot cider and sliced sweet bread. I do believe the adults may have something added to their cider. Of course, there is the Christmas Eve service at the church."

"Camille, Dante and I will be escorting you and Martha to the service."

"After supper at my house," Martha added.

"You must let me help, Martha. I'm horrible at sitting around and not contributing."

"Of course. It won't be fancy, but your help is appreciated. Oh, I almost forgot. The women at the Pelletier ranch have sewn a Christmas quilt. It will be auctioned off on the second night of the choral. I heard it's beautiful."

"Well, we must go both nights." She looked at her brother.

"Of course, Camille." It would be his pleasure to hear Martha sing both evenings. He had no doubt Camilla would leave after the second performance with a quilt over her arm.

Sean MacLaren, a leather bag tied to the back of his saddle, rode with purpose alongside Noah Brandt. The livery owner had arrived early at the MacLaren ranch south of Splendor to seek Sean's help.

With a university degree, plus years of experience on the family ranch in northern California, his skills were becoming increasingly recognized. Even more skeptical ranchers, who didn't understand the breadth of Sean's experience, were beginning to seek him out.

Tugging up his heavy coat to warn off the cold, he looked at Noah and shouted over the brisk wind, "How many horses are affected?"

"Can't say for certain. I isolated five horses. There could be more." Noah's jaw tightened, his gaze intent on the horizon ahead. It would take longer than either wanted for them to reach his livery in Splendor. The fact Noah came for Sean said a great deal about his confidence in the new veterinarian.

Neither commented when the town came into sight. Increasing the pace, they urged their horses to move faster through the snow.

Sean had a notion of what ailed Noah's animals before he dismounted at the livery. He'd been reading about the illness in a letter from a fellow veterinarian who'd attended university with Sean. The doctor now lived in upper New York state. The two shared information and discoveries by mail.

Dismounting, he removed the bag tied to his saddle. Noah showed him to the first horse in a line of stalls.

"This gelding started acting ill three days ago. The following day, the other four horses showed the same signs. I should've gone after you sooner."

Sean nodded, listening as he examined the gelding. Opening the bag, he took out the mercury thermometer, similar to those used by the doctor at the clinic. He next retrieved a small tub of lard. Last, he removed a clean cloth.

Noah's gentle hand and patient manner calmed the gelding while Sean completed the procedure. A few minutes later, he checked the reading.

"It's high, Noah. I want to check the other four, plus one or two you haven't quarantined."

An hour later, Sean put his equipment away. "I believe we're looking at equine influenza. The high fevers, deep coughing, rapid breathing, and general lethargy are common symptoms of this illness. You were smart to separate the sick horses. Only five are infected. Doesn't mean the others won't contract the illness."

"What do I do about them?"

"You're already isolating the infected horses. Keep their water clean and make sure they have plenty to drink. Rest is critical. Do you have horse blankets?"

Noah gave him a blank look.

"Some stables back east use blankets in the winter. You could rig something by using a wool blanket placed over their backs, then securing them with rope. The warmth may help bring down their temperatures. I can help you."

Noah rubbed a hand over his forehead. "Thanks, Doc. I promised to take town children and those at the orphanage on wagon rides before Christmas. Should I cancel?"

"Are you able to use uninfected horses?"

"Possibly. Many aren't mine. The owners stable them here."

"What about talking with Dax and Luke Pelletier? They have several wagons and a large number of horses."

"All I need are horses that aren't sick."

"Take care of your horses, Noah. I'll ride to the Pelletier ranch. When did you plan the rides?"

Martha attached the pendant of an enameled angel around her neck before checking herself in the mirror. Adjusting it, she slipped on her heavy coat. She looked at the mantel clock, which sat on a bookcase she'd purchased the previous summer.

The knock on her door triggered fluttering sensations in her stomach. Certain it was Cole, she opened it.

"Oh, Dante. What a wonderful surprise." Looking beyond him, disappointment must've shown on her face.

"Papa had to go to the jail with Aunt Camilla. He asked me to walk with you to the church."

"What a fine idea." Picking up her reticule, she closed the door. She hid a surprised chuckle when Dante held out his arm. Slipping her arm through his, she smiled. "You are a true gentleman."

Dante took a route down her street to the end before turning right. Two blocks in front of them stood the community building. The church was to the right.

Light streamed from the inside of each building, illuminating the wreaths and bows attached to the outside walls. Several wagons were parked outside.

"Will there be a lot of people, Miss van Plew?"

"I hope so. Do you remember me telling you at breakfast there'll be a bake sale?"

His face lit up. "Yes. Will there be candy?"

"I do believe there will be. Candy, cookies, sweet breads, pies, and cakes."

"I like all of them."

"You may have to pick just one. After all, we have to leave something for the other families, right?"

"I guess so."

"Dante!"

They looked toward the shout, seeing Lena, holding a squirming Emma, and Jackson. Dante waved.

"Can we go over there, Miss van Plew?"

"I don't know why not."

They crossed the street, walking along the outside of the church until they reached them.

"Good evening, Lena. You have your hands full."

Lena laughed, placing a kiss on Emma's cheek. "She's three and can walk everywhere inside and around our house. For some reason, she doesn't want to be put down in town. Not even in the jail when Gabe is there. She'll let him hold her, just not put her down. It is tiring."

"Will she let me hold her?"

"We can try."

Lena held Emma out and into Martha's open arms. The young girl smiled, wrapping her arms around Martha's neck.

"When you get tired, just hand her back."

"Will Gabe be coming?"

"Tonight and tomorrow." Lena smiled. She looked at Dante. "He, Cole, and Camilla are making some decisions about what to do next."

"Excuse me?"

"About returning to New York."

"I'm sorry, Lena. I don't know what you're talking about."

"Oh, my. You don't know."

"Don't know what?"

"It's not my place to tell you, but it's a little late now. Cole, Dante, and Camilla may have to return east. Their father passed away yesterday."

Chapter Twenty-One

Martha stood next to Lena in their line of women. Both were members of the Splendor choral, a group of men and women who presented singing performances a few times each year. The two Christmas concerts would conclude their year.

They were halfway through their program when Lena nudged Martha, then nodded toward the back of the church. Gabe, Cole, and Camilla stood near the back door, watching. Martha made eye contact with Cole, who gave a slight nod back.

Jackson held Emma on his lap in the front row. Dante sat next to them. The spot allowed Emma to see her mother, which kept her quiet.

The group sang four more songs before concluding to loud applause from the audience. The singers walked toward their friends and family before everyone made the short trip to the community room. Inside, the church women had spread out baked goods for the sale. One table held pots of coffee, with hot milk warming on the cookstove for chocolate. The drinks were offered at no cost.

Cole and Camilla waited for Martha by the back door. He spotted her talking with another of the choral members and raised his hand. She lifted hers in return, ended the conversation, and joined them.

"Lena told me what happened. I'm so sorry about your father."

Camilla gave a solemn nod. "Thank you, Martha."

Cole reached out his hand. She hesitated a moment before slipping her fingers through his.

"What are your plans?"

"We sent a return telegram to Mother," Cole answered.

"Before leaving New York, Mother and I made sure all Father's affairs were in order. We knew he wouldn't be with us much longer." Camilla exhaled a slow breath. "I'll have to return."

"Wait for Mother's response, Cam."

"I'm not sure she's strong enough to get through this alone."

Dante ran up to them, stopping in front of Cole. "Are you coming, Papa?"

He set a hand on his son's shoulder. "Why don't you show us where to go."

Taking them to the community building, Dante stopped in front of a table filled with candy and baked goods. Each one had a hand-labeled sign indicating the price.

"Are you hungry?"

Dante nodded vigorously at Cole. "May I have two?"

"Sure. Which ones?"

"Those, please." He pointed to a plate of sugar cookies and another with molasses cookies.

"Hello, Deputy Santori." A young woman he recognized from the Eagle's Nest smiled at him.

"Good evening, Sally. I'd like four sugar and four molasses."

"Excellent choices. May Covington made all the cookies and breads."

Cole turned to his sister. "May is the pastry chef at the Eagle's Nest. She's married to Caleb, another deputy."

"Her desserts are incredible, Camilla." Martha's attention moved to the sweet breads.

"Here you are, Deputy." He took the cookies, handing one of each to his sister, son, and Martha. "Thank you, Sally." He gave her money and was ready to leave when Martha spoke up.

"I'll have a loaf of fruit bread and one gingerbread."

"And what will you do with two loaves?" Cole asked, taking one loaf from her hand so she could eat a cookie.

She leaned toward him, lowering her voice. "If Camilla must travel back east, slices of these would be nice to take along. Whatever is left, I'll share."

"With?" He finished his sugar cookie and bit into the molasses one.

"I'll have to think about that." Martha's eyes twinkled.

"Think about Dante and me while you're deciding." Cole's grin had her chuckling.

Camilla joked to Dante about ruining his supper with cookies before touching Cole's arm. "Perhaps I should check the telegraph office to see if Mother replied."

"I'll go with you. Martha, may Dante stay with you?"

"Of course. We'll be here a while longer, then walk to my house. I made chicken stew. There's enough for all of us."

"Thank you." He bent down, as if meaning to kiss her, then pulled back. "Probably should wait until we're alone."

Her face showed disappointment, though both of them knew it was the right decision. "Don't forget."

"I won't."

"What do you think, Cole?" Camilla stood next to him after reading the telegram from their mother.

"I'm not sure. It's clear she doesn't want to wait for Father's funeral until we return to New York."

"We? I didn't think you'd be able to leave."

"I didn't want to say anything in front of Dante and Martha until Mother replied. I'm not sure what to make of this." He held up the telegram. "The other siblings should arrive in time."

"I would hope so."

"You don't think they will?"

Her mouth formed a thin line. "Three of our six siblings will be there for Mother."

"Not for Father?"

"Columbus. You better than anyone know how difficult Father could be and how harsh in his criticism. He wasn't this way just with you. Although, you were the most frequent target of his anger. She may not have rescued us from his temper, but Mother did hold everyone together."

Cole considered her words. He'd never considered how his father treated others in the family. "What do you want to do?"

"She was clear about not delaying Father's funeral. I do understand. The plans were finalized months ago when the doctor advised him of his short future. If Mother doesn't require our support, there's no reason to go."

"We should send Mother a telegram confirming we won't be returning in the near future. Would you prefer I send it?"

Camilla shook her head. "No. I'll do it."

"I'll wait for you."

"No, Columbus. I'm going to sit here for a few minutes to gather my thoughts. Find Dante and Martha. That's where you should be." She walked to the wooden bench inside the office and sat down. He stood over her, contemplating staying. After a while, he kissed her on the cheek and left.

Cole stepped outside to find a light snow falling. Shoving his hands into his pockets, he maneuvered the large pockets of icy mud to cross the street. Reaching the opposite boardwalk, he took his time, his father playing in his mind.

He'd finally obtained the truth about his adoption. His father hadn't tried to soften the news. The explanation had been delivered as if the senior Santori were presenting a report to investors. It had stung, even if his father had answered many questions weighing on Cole for years.

Continuing along the boardwalk, he crossed the street once more, stopping at the jail. Lantern light poured through the window. Not a surprise, as it was Morgan, Jonas, and Tucker's job to man the jail at night. He didn't enter.

"Time to find your boy and go home," Cole whispered to himself as he continued to Martha's house. He shoved aside the images of his father on his deathbed, replacing each one with pictures of Martha. Martha alone. Martha with Dante. Martha with Cole. A smile grew fuller with each image.

Cole knew he was going to marry her one day. Soon, if he could find the courage to ask.

Camilla sat long after sending up a series of prayers while formulating a telegram to her mother. Guilt, understanding, confusion, and finally peace settled over her.

She sent the message to New York, knowing there'd be no response until the following day. When she'd apologized for keeping him late, Bernie Griggs bobbed up and down on the balls of his feet.

"Don't worry about it, Miss Santori. I always stay longer the week before Christmas. A few days afterward, too. People need to communicate with family this time of year. Right?"

"You are so right, Mr. Griggs."

"Bernie." He smiled. "Nobody calls me Mr. Griggs. Not even Reverend Paige."

"All right. Well, goodnight, Bernie."

"Goodnight, Miss Santori."

Stepping outside, she pulled up the collar of her heavy coat. The temperature had dropped again while she'd been inside the office. Glancing around, she noticed wagons leaving the community building, as well as riders on their horses heading home.

She'd been surprised at the wondrous performance by the choral. Who would've thought a small town in the frontier would hold such incredible talent? It had humbled her. From tonight on, she wouldn't underestimate the people of Splendor.

Passing the general store, she stopped for a minute to look in the window. Stan Petermann's hand-carved nativity scene opened her eyes to another aspect of the town. Many creative people had settled here. From May Covington's incredible desserts to Allie Coulter's exquisite dresses and Stan's carvings.

Continuing her path to the St. James Hotel, Camilla wondered what special talent she possessed. She was a proficient cook, with an ability to mend, if not create dresses. Carving was quite beyond her, as was drawing of any kind. She couldn't hold a tune, though she could play the piano.

What she could do was manage a household. No wonder she'd never attracted the interest of a man for more than a few weeks. She'd long ago given up her dream of marrying and having several children. Seeing so many happy families brought back the disappointment she'd buried so long ago.

"Lass! Wait up."

Her steps slowed for a moment before she continued walking. Surely, whoever had called out hadn't meant her.

"Wait up, lass."

This time, she stopped, making a slow turn to face the man who moved swiftly on the boardwalk. She didn't recognize him and felt a slight moment of fear.

"A lass shouldn't be walking alone at night. Especially on such a cold one. I'm Sean MacLaren, the veterinarian in Splendor."

"It's a pleasure to meet you, Doctor MacLaren. I'm Miss Camilla Santori."

"Aye, I heard Cole's sister was in town. May I walk you home?"

"I'm staying just up the street at the St. James. I don't want to inconvenience you."

A smile lit up his face. "It's never an inconvenience to walk beside a bonnie lass."

"Are you teasing me?" She studied his face, finding his square jaw, straight nose, and emerald green eyes quite appealing.

He pressed his open palm against his heart. "Never." He held out his arm. "I'd welcome the honor of escorting you home tonight, Miss Santori."

She hesitated only a moment before slipping her arm through his.

Chapter Twenty-Two

"He is a fascinating man." Camilla sipped coffee the following morning, feeling an unusual sense of anticipation. "Did you know he attended university in Scotland?"

Across the table, Martha set down her cup. "I heard as much from Selina MacLaren. She's married to Bram MacLaren. As I understand it, he's Sean's cousin. The MacLarens are quite a large family."

Camilla cut into the large slice of ham, placing a bite in her mouth. She appeared to be contemplating something of great weight. Swallowing, she idly took another sip of coffee.

"Sean mentioned most of his family lives on a ranch in northern California."

"I don't know much about them. My understanding is they raise cattle and breed horses. Similar to what the Pelletier brothers do. I learned this from Rachel Pelletier. They partner with Bram and Thane MacLaren to supply the Army with horses."

"Interesting, and so different than the work my acquaintances do in New York. It's a different world out here."

Martha laughed. "I thought the same when I moved here. After a time, it has become just another part of life in this part of the country."

"Are you glad you moved here?"

"Hmmm." Martha glanced out the window of the Eagle's Nest restaurant before looking at Camilla. "I love it here. It suits me better than Boston. There, I had to listen to my family saying something was inappropriate or not suitable for me. I've never heard the same here. Women live life as they choose, without fear of being judged. Though, I will say, life out here is more difficult. Single women, without education or specific skills, have a hard time making a living."

"Cole tells me you are the administrator for the orphanage. What a marvelous position."

Finishing her eggs, Martha picked up her cup, taking the last sip. "I'm the interim administrator. The committee who started the orphanage is searching for my replacement."

"You aren't interested in continuing?"

"There is something else I'd rather do."

Camilla tilted her head. "What is that?"

Martha studied the other woman a moment. "I want to write."

"Really? How interesting. What would you write about?"

"Life in Splendor. What it's like as a woman living in the west."

"What a marvelous idea. Have you written before?"

"Nothing beyond normal correspondence. I don't know if any publisher would be interested in my writing."

"Don't let that stop you, Martha. Write what's in your heart. I may be able to help you find a publisher. My father had a broad range of acquaintances." Camilla paused a moment, realizing she'd spoken of him in the past tense. Releasing a breath, she straightened in her chair. "I've met many of them. Mother always hated acting as a hostess during his many social obligations."

"You enjoyed them?"

"More than Mother. I've always enjoyed learning about people. Over time, my social circle became quite broad. Have you heard of Little, Brown, and Company, or Roberts Brothers?"

Martha's eyes widened. "Of course."

"I know gentlemen at both companies. They're known for publishing female authors. I'd start with them."

"You hardly know me, Camilla. What if my writing is dreadful?"

"Columbus is an excellent judge of character. From what I've seen, my brother is quite fond of you, Martha. There isn't much more I need to know."

Cole read another telegram from his mother. Handing it to Camilla, he blinked away the unaccustomed moisture in his eyes. Reading it twice, she folded the paper, holding it out toward Cole.

"You keep it with the others, Cam. Mother was quite firm about us not going back. Will you stay here?" He opened the door of the telegraph office. She walked past him onto the boardwalk.

"At least for a while. I'll make a decision in the spring. If I do leave, I'll travel west. I'd like to see California."

"California, huh? You should speak with the MacLarens before you go." They continued their walk, heading to Chinatown. Cole knew she'd enjoy visiting the various shops.

"I met Sean MacLaren last evening."

"Where?"

She explained her walk after sending the telegram to their mother. How Sean had called out to her, chastising her for walking alone at night.

"He told me a woman shouldn't walk alone on such a night."

"Sean was right. Did he walk you back to the hotel?"

"He did. Sean got us a table in the restaurant. That's when I realized I'd never had supper. Neither had he. We ate and talked. He's quite fascinating."

"Is he?"

"You know him. What do you think about him, Columbus?"

"I don't know much about Sean. I know he's a trained veterinarian. He's Bram and Thane MacLaren's cousin. That's the extent of my knowledge."

"You know their family has a large ranch in California, right?"

"That's my understanding."

"Sean's family sent him to Highland Society's Veterinary School in Edinburgh. It's a world-renowned university. When he returned, a friend and fellow graduate of the school came with him. The family hadn't planned to send him out here. Sean made his own case for coming to Splendor."

"He obviously won."

"Yes. I'm certain Sean can be quite persuasive."

Cole noted a flash of color on his sister's face. "Did he ask to see you again?"

They turned a corner. Before them was Grant Street and Chinatown.

"How interesting," she said, avoiding his question.

"Cam. Did Sean ask to see you again?"

"Yes. He's escorting me to the second choral performance tonight. Will you be there with Dante?"

"Yes."

"I thought you would. You should ask Martha to marry you, Columbus."

Chuckling, he stared down at his boots. "Why is that?"

"You love her. She loves you and Dante. Do you need to know more?"

His gaze rose to meet hers. "How do you know she loves me?"

"Women know these things. Besides, she is beautiful, educated, interesting, and plans to stay in Splendor."

"Martha told you she's staying?"

"She loves it here. It's a small town. Do you want to miss your chance and be forced to see her in Splendor with another man?"

He didn't respond as they continued into Chinatown. The question stuck in his head the rest of the day.

The question snuck up on him again while he and Dante listened to the choral that evening. They sat next to Camilla. Sean sat on her other side. On the other side of Dante were Jackson and Gabe. Emma slept in his arms.

Lena and Martha stood in the same positions as the previous night. If he closed his eyes, Cole believed he could hear Martha's clear voice. As his wise sister had said to him that afternoon, she was beautiful. Could he stand to watch her with someone else? Unconsciously, he shook his head.

"Papa?" Dante's whisper stopped his thoughts on Martha with another man.

"Hmmm?"

"Can I have cookies again after Miss van Plew is finished?"

Cole nodded, which satisfied Dante. It didn't stop him from thinking about proposing marriage to Martha.

The thought of a life with her had been on his mind for quite some time. He didn't need much encouragement.

When Dante came into his life, Cole had wanted time to become familiar with his son. Dante, who'd lost his mother and grandparents, required assurance Cole loved and wanted him. Those accomplished, he could now concentrate on convincing Martha of his feelings for her.

His thoughts on her ended when the audience stood. Applause, along with a few whistles, signaled the end of the performance. If anyone asked him what the Christmas choral had sung, he wouldn't have been able to answer.

Dante took his hand, tugging Cole toward Martha. She stood near the door, talking with Lena. A burst of laughter erupted from deep in her throat, spontaneous and pure. He loved hearing the sound coming from a woman who fought to maintain a certain level of decorum. Perhaps the essence of Splendor was catching ahold of her.

"Miss van Plew!"

She turned toward Cole, looking down at Dante. "Good evening. Did you enjoy the singing?"

"You were really good."

"You could hear me?"

He gave several emphatic nods, causing Martha and Cole to laugh.

"I've promised Dante he could have another cookie. Would you care to come with us?"

"I'd love to." She accepted his proffered arm with a grin. "Did you enjoy the performance?"

"I did."

"Beauty DeBell's solo was excellent."

"Hawke's wife can sing." Cole winced. He didn't remember Beauty's solo.

Crossing from the church to the community building, they felt the light snow on their faces. Cole hoped if a new storm hit Splendor, it would wait until after Christmas.

They entered the community building to hear music from a local band led by Stan Petermann. "I don't believe Stan ever sleeps." Martha stopped to enjoy a rousing Jingle Bells.

Dante and most of the children sang along while the adults clapped. Cole watched his son and Martha, not recalling another time when he'd felt so content.

Chapter Twenty-Three

Cole used his gloved hand to brush the snow from a bench outside the schoolhouse. Dante had spent the night with Jackson Evans, giving him a morning free to think.

He would be taking Dante to the church that afternoon to catch one of the wagon rides Noah offered. Three trips were the usual, and all were full of both children and adults. Cole had always thought it odd. Even people without wagons rode on them several times a year.

Christmas rides were special. That's what everyone had told him. He hadn't taken one since arriving in Splendor. Maybe they were special. Perhaps this afternoon he'd find out.

Resting against the back of the bench, he stretched out his legs. Two days before Christmas and the sun's rays were almost too warm. Unbuttoning his coat, he let out a relieved sigh at the cooling breeze.

Cole had wrestled all night with his feelings for Martha. Or rather, what he hoped her feelings were for him. There was another, equally important concern that nagged at him.

Did she want to be a mother to Dante? Would Dante be comfortable with another woman taking his mother's place?

Cole already knew about her skills working with children. Her calm manner made conversation easy. He'd seen her discipline unruly boys and girls. She wasn't too harsh or lenient. Dante seemed to like her, but would he accept her if she lived in their home?

Those conversations would need to happen before making any decision about marriage.

"I thought it was you." Martha stopped in front of him. She gestured to the bench. "Do you mind if I join you?"

Standing, he brushed a kiss across her cheek. "I'd enjoy your company." Once she was settled, he sat down next to her. "Weren't you going to the orphanage this morning?"

"I'm going later this morning. The children want to go on one of Noah's wagon rides. He's agreed to an early one so it doesn't interrupt the ones already planned. I assume Dante is still with Lena and the children."

"I'll go for him in an hour."

"If there's enough room in the wagon, he's welcome to ride along with the orphanage children."

"Thank you, Martha. I'm certain he'd enjoy it more than staying in the jail while I make my rounds."

She placed a hand on his arm. "When I'm in town, he can stay with me when school is out."

He smiled at her, remembering his thoughts of a few minutes earlier. "That's generous of you, Martha."

"Not so much. I enjoy his company. Dante is bright and curious. He's easy to be around, Cole. I wonder what his father was like."

"I never asked. Evelyn was bright, the same as Dante. And easy to be around. While Dante is outgoing and has many friends, Evelyn was quiet with few close friends. While I knew her, she mentioned just one friend. The same woman who delivered the letter to Camilla."

"You and this woman were her only friends?"

"The woman, yes."

Martha chuckled. "A woman wouldn't leave her son to someone who she didn't consider a friend."

"I'm certain you're right."

"Do you wonder why you have Dante and not Evelyn's female friend?"

"According to Camilla, the woman didn't have the money to take care of him."

"Assuming there were funds left for you to use for Dante, it seems an unconvincing excuse."

"There was nothing."

Martha's eyes flashed in surprise. "What?"

"Camilla obtained background on the family. The house was sold to pay off debt owed by Evelyn's parents. Their meager savings were also used for debt. Camilla received Dante's clothes, toys, books, a desk and chair, and a few other items."

"Did she know about your family?"

"Yes."

"Then it does make sense. She knew you would have the funds to raise him, while her other friend did not. What a sad situation." She laid a hand on his arm. "You are a good man, Cole."

"I don't know about being good," he scoffed. "I did make the offer to raise him, and I'm honored she made my promise known to her friend. He could've ended up in an orphanage."

"My experience with orphanages back east is scarce. All I know is what I've been told. It would've been a miracle if he'd ended up in one of the few good ones."

He moved closer, taking her hand in his. "Do you hope to have children of your own someday, Martha?"

She tilted her head, studying his face. After a time, she looked away. "Yes, I would love to have children. Five like Dante would be perfect."

"Mama, will there be singing?" Joel Heaton's wide, inquisitive eyes met his mother's.

"I do not know. If not, perhaps you can start singing and others will join you." Dorinda adjusted her bulky wool skirt on the wagon's seat.

"What would I sing?"

"What is your favorite Christmas song?"

A smile broke across his face. "Jingle Bells."

"That is your answer."

"Will you and Uncle Spencer go with me?" Joel's gaze moved to his uncle, who drove the wagon, then shifted back to his mother.

"If there is room, I am sure Mr. Brandt will allow us to ride in the wagon with you."

Dorinda regretted not allowing Joel to go the night before with the rest of the children from the Pelletier ranch. Concern over Jared still being in Splendor stopped her. Spencer's offer to take them to town today had eased her fears.

The sight greeting them as they rode down Frontier Street was quite spectacular. Most posts along the boardwalk were wrapped in pine boughs and an occasional bow. A few businesses had signs in windows wishing everyone a Merry Christmas. Several pine wreaths with red ribbons and strands of popcorn and cranberries hung in the front window of Splendor Emporium.

Joel kept twisting from one side to the other so as not to miss anything. Someone in the Dixie Saloon played a rousing version of Jingle Bells.

Joel pointed toward the swinging doors. "Mama. Listen."

Reaching the end of the street, Spencer stopped next to another wagon outside the community building. Noah stood close by, talking to a tall, slender man wearing a fur hat.

Jumping down, Spencer helped Joel and Dorinda to the ground. "I'll find out when Noah is leaving. Do you want to wait inside the church or community building?"

Dorinda glanced about, seeing the man with the fur hat walk away, then shook her head. "We will wait for you."

She kept her gaze moving from the St. James to the Emporium to McCall's restaurant across the street. A man emerged from the general store. Her body went rigid. Jared looked away from them, toward the other end of town. She reached out to take Joel's hand, tugging him closer to Noah's wagon.

"Mama, you're hurting my hand."

Loosening her grip, Dorinda never shifted her attention from Jared. She knelt down behind the wagon when he turned in their direction.

Spencer called her name, but she didn't move, shushing Joel with a finger. She hated the fear in her son's eyes. For now, there was nothing she could do to reassure him.

Dorinda could hear boots crunching through icy snow. Her heart pounded wildly until Spencer appeared next to them.

"What is it, Dorie?"

"Jared came out of the general store. Is he still there?"

She watched her brother study the street, taking his time. "I don't see him." Reaching down, he helped her up. "I'd hoped he would've given up and gone home. Dax told me the sheriff spoke to Jared. Gabe warned him to leave if he didn't have business in town."

"Jared will not quit until he is forced to go. He cannot be away from the farm much longer."

"I don't know what he expects will happen. You've made it clear your marriage is over."

"He has a great amount of pride. I believe Jared wishes he had not taken a second wife. She is not a good person. It is too late to change his mind."

Spencer continued to watch the street. "He could divorce her."

Deep sadness showed in her eyes. "He will not."

"Mama?"

Though she still held Joel's hand, she'd forgotten he could hear their conversation. "Yes?"

"Is Papa here?"

"Yes."

"Can I see him?"

Closing her eyes, she shook her head. "I am sorry, Joel. You cannot."

The tense moment broke at the sound of children laughing. Dorinda spotted Martha driving a wagon filled with boys and girls.

"Noah said he is taking children from the orphanage on a ride. Joel is welcome to go with them."

"What do you think, Joel?" Dorinda waited.

"I don't know them, Mama."

"This is your chance to meet them."

Spencer knelt in front of Joel. "Noah told me Dante Santori is going to join them. You'll like him. I'll speak with Miss van Plew."

Dorinda continued to watch for Jared while Spencer spoke with Martha. They walked around Noah's wagon toward them.

"Good afternoon, Dorinda."

"Hello, Miss van Plew."

"Please call me Martha. Joel is welcome to join us." She smiled down at him. "It won't be a long ride, as Noah is doing this before his other rides. We packed food and containers of hot chocolate. The children love to sing. I understand you know Jingle Bells.”

Joel nodded.

Martha held out her hand. “Excellent. We can always use another voice. You’re welcome, too, Dorinda.”

“Go, Dorinda,” Spencer said. “It will give me time to talk to the sheriff. Noah won’t let anything happen to you or Joel.”

“Amy and Rose aren’t on the ride. I would love to have another woman with me.”

Dorinda chuckled. “It does sound fun. Joel, what do you think?”

“I want to go.”

She looked back at Martha. “That is my answer, too.”

Chapter Twenty-Four

Christmas Eve Morning

Cole rode to the orphanage early in the morning. Dante rode beside him, flashing a smile at his father every few minutes. They'd been blessed with a warm sun and no snow for a few days, making the ride an easy one.

Martha had returned the children to the orphanage later the previous evening, after treating them to an early supper at the boardinghouse. Cole and Dante had been invited to join them. He'd accepted. It had been a good decision, as Suzanne had set aside a cake big enough for everyone.

Martha had stayed the night at the orphanage instead of making the trip back to town. He'd been surprised how much he missed not spending part of the evening with her.

Cole awoke with purpose the morning of Christmas Eve. He hadn't tried to talk himself out of the decision the previous night. Nor did he spend time examining the choice that morning.

The orphanage came into sight as they completed the last bend in the trail. The two-story, white structure appeared elegant and more imposing at this time of day.

Dismounting, he waited for Dante to join him before taking the steps to the front door. He nodded at his son to knock. Teddy opened it a crack. A smile spread across his face.

"Who is it, Teddy?"

Cole's stomach tightened when he recognized Martha's voice.

"Cole. Dante. What a wonderful surprise. Come in. We're just sitting down to a rather late breakfast. You must join us."

Removing their hats, they followed Martha and Teddy to the kitchen. Amy set a large platter of hotcakes on the table as they entered. Rose set down a second one, equally as large. Eggs, ham, and a bowl of frypan potatoes were waiting to be devoured by the hungry children.

"Sit beside me, Dante." Teddy motioned to the end of the table.

Cole pulled out Martha's chair, eliciting snickers from around the table. Amy set two baskets of biscuits down before she and Rose took their places.

"Cole, would you say the blessing?"

All heads bowed over their clasped hands. The blessing was brief. When amen was spoken by all, the children began filling their plates.

Cole's plate held half as much as Dante's. "Hope you can eat all of that, son."

"I can." His enthusiasm made Cole chuckle.

"What brought you all the way out here?"

"I would think it obvious." He cut a slice of ham.

"Tell me."

"Dante wanted to play with the children. The other boys in town are with their parents."

Her face fell before she caught herself. "An excellent reason."

"I wanted to see you."

"That's an even better reason."

"I thought so."

Her laughter caught in his chest. The same as it always did. Cole knew he'd never tire of hearing her laugh. The same as everything else about her.

"Bobby. Don't take food from Hattie's plate."

"She isn't going to eat it."

"Not if you take it. Concentrate on your own plate, then you may ask Hattie if she's finished. If so, you may eat what's left."

Bobby hung his head. "All right…"

"You are a tough woman, Martha."

"But fair. That's what Amy and Rose tell me."

It was his turn to chuckle. "I agree with them."

Conversation slowed as they ate. Cole's thoughts went to the night before and his conversation with Dante.

He'd asked what his son thought of Martha. To his surprise, Dante told him he liked her and that Cole should marry her. He'd almost choked on his coffee. Children always seemed to come straight to the point.

Cole looked at Dante, who sat a couple seats away. He must've felt his father's gaze on him because he shifted in his chair, smiling at Cole. Then he nodded toward Martha, as if nudging his father.

He didn't need any more pressure than what he already felt. Certainly not from an eight-year-old. Cole ignored Dante's urging. He'd do this in his own time.

"What will you and the children do today?"

"Nothing different than any other day they don't have school. Except for tonight. Rose, Amy, and I will be taking the children to Christmas Eve services at the church. Some have never been to one." She picked up her cup. "I'm looking forward to Dorinda starting. If her husband would just leave town."

"Gabe spoke to Heaton again. He's leaving on today's stage west."

"That's wonderful news, Cole. She'll feel free to move into town."

"Gabe sent a deputy to the Pelletier ranch to let Dorinda know. And to deliver a letter her husband wrote to her."

Martha set the cup down. "I hope the contents won't change her mind."

He shrugged. "Whatever happens, it will be her choice. Do you have a few minutes to talk in private?"

"Of course. I'll let Rose and Amy know." The legs of the chair scraped against the wood floor when she stood. "We can talk in the office."

It took no time at all to carry their plates to the counter by the sink. Martha spoke to Amy and Rose, nodding at Cole to join her in the office.

Closing the door behind him, he turned to face her. After making the decision and practicing what he'd say, he now found it hard to start.

She stood close to the desk, hands clasped in front of her, waiting. Her eyes widened when he walked to her, taking her hands in his.

"I don't know how else to say this, so, well... I'll just get it out." Cole winced at the sharp sound of his voice. "Let me start again."

"For heaven's sake, Cole. Don't drag this out. Say whatever is bothering you."

He flinched at what she might be thinking. Squeezing her hands in his, he decided to do as she suggested.

"I love you, Martha. So does Dante. We can't imagine a life without you, and I couldn't tolerate you being with another man." He saw her lips part and continued. "If you feel the same, and I believe you do, let's get married."

Surprise, then amusement showed on her face as the seconds ticked by. She didn't respond, making him wonder if he'd made a mistake. He was ready to try again when she ended his misery.

"Cole Santori. In the history of marriage proposals, that must be one of the strangest. And one of the most honest." Pulling one hand free, she cupped his cheek, her gaze on his. "You and Dante are the two most important people in my life. I love both of you. So very much." Releasing a deep breath, she smiled. "I would be honored, thrilled, ecstatic, and overjoyed to be your wife."

Wrapping her arms around his neck, they kissed, then kissed again, until both ran out of breath.

Epilogue

Splendor Church, Christmas Eve

Cole slid off his horse before helping Martha to the ground. She'd refused to ride to town in the wagon without him next to her. He'd agreed.

Dante dismounted, joy radiating from his young face. Cole and Martha hadn't been fast enough to announce their engagement before Dante blurted out the news to Amy, Rose, and the other children. Bedlam broke out for several minutes, until the boys and girls dressed in heavy coats, boots, and hats, and ran outside. Dante followed right behind them.

The two waited outside the church until everyone from the orphanage filed inside. Camilla stood just inside, waiting for them.

"I think you should tell her, Cole."

"All right." Kissing her cheek, he reached for her hand. Even through their gloves, he felt a surge of excitement.

"I wondered where you two were. Was there a problem at the orphanage?"

He bent to kiss Camilla's cheek. "Not at all. There is some news, however."

"Tell me quick. Sean is holding seats for us."

This time, Cole didn't stumble for words. "Martha has agreed to do me the honor of becoming my wife."

"What?" Her voice screeched with delight, drawing the attention of those around them. "Oh, that is wonderful news. Fabulous, in fact." She hugged Martha, startling both of them before turning to her brother. "You made a wise choice, little brother."

"Are you coming?" Sean stood a few feet away, his gaze moving between the three of them. "I have Bram and Selina holding our seats."

"Yes, we are," Camilla all but shouted. Slipping her arm through Sean's, she beamed almost as much as Martha as they took their seats.

A moment later, Sean reached across the women to shake Cole's hand. "Well done, lad."

News of their betrothal spread as the choir sang the opening hymns. Several heads turned toward them, mouthing congratulations. Those in the row behind them clasped Cole on the shoulder while the women whispered their excitement to Martha.

Reverend Paige's message was an uplifting tale of new beginnings. He spoke from the Bible, relaying the message of Jesus's miraculous birth, reminding everyone of how miracles happened every day in Splendor.

His booming voice sounded inside the church walls. "Be open to them and they will surely come!"

Finishing with an inspirational prayer, he lifted his gaze to the parishioners. He nodded at a woman in the first row. Regal, with her almost white blonde hair glistening in the candlelight, Beauty DeBell began to sing.

Silent night. Holy night.
All is calm, all is bright
round yon Virgin Mother and Child,
Holy infant so tender and mild,
Sleep in Heavenly peace...
Sleep in Heavenly peace!

Cole squeezed Martha's hand. Leaning toward her, he whispered in her ear. "You, beautiful Martha, truly are my miracle."

Traditional Pound Cake

Ingredients:

- 1 pound of butter
- 1 pound of sugar
- 1 pound of flour
- 10 large eggs
- 1 teaspoon of vanilla extract
- 1/2 teaspoon of lemon extract (or the grated zest of one lemon)

Instructions:

1. Preheat your oven to 325°F (163°C). Grease and flour a large cake pan.
2. In a large mixing bowl, cream together the butter and sugar. This can be done with a wooden spoon or a hand mixer. Cream until the mixture is light and fluffy.
3. Add the eggs one at a time, beating well after each addition.
4. Sift the flour and add it gradually to the butter and egg mixture. Mix until the batter is smooth and well combined.
5. Stir in the vanilla extract and lemon extract (or lemon zest) to flavor the cake.
6. Pour the cake batter into the prepared pan and smooth the top.
7. Bake in the preheated oven for about 1 to 1.5 hours. Check for doneness by inserting a toothpick into

the center of the cake; it should come out clean when the cake is done.

8. Once the cake is baked, remove it from the oven and allow it to cool in the pan for about 10-15 minutes. Then, remove the cake from the pan and let it cool completely on a wire rack.

Modified for contemporary baking from an original 1870s recipe, this pound cake is a classic. Did you know it's called a "pound cake" because it traditionally used a pound each of butter, sugar, flour, and eggs?

Hope you enjoy this delicious slice of history!

Enjoying the **Redemption Mountain** books? Here's another series you might want to read.

MacLarens of Boundary Mountain historical western romance series.

If you want to keep current on all my preorders, new releases, and other happenings, sign up for my newsletter: http://www.shirleendavies.com/contact-me.html

A Note from Shirleen

Thank you for taking the time to read Whisper Lake, Another Very Splendor Christmas!

If you enjoyed it, please consider telling your friends or posting a short review. Word of mouth is an author's best friend and much appreciated.

I care about quality, so if you find something in error, please contact me via email at
shirleen@shirleendavies.com

Books by Shirleen Davies

<u>Historical Western Romances</u>

Redemption Mountain
MacLarens of Fire Mountain Historical
MacLarens of Boundary Mountain

<u>Contemporary Western Romance</u>

Cowboys of Whistle Rock Ranch
MacLarens of Fire Mountain Contemporary
Macklins of Whiskey Bend

Romantic Suspense

Eternal Brethren Military Romantic Suspense
Peregrine Bay Romantic Suspense

Find all of my books at:
http://www.shirleendavies.com/books.html

About Shirleen

Shirleen Davies writes romance—historical and contemporary western romance, and romantic suspense. She grew up in Southern California, attended Oregon State University, and has degrees from San Diego State University and the University of Maryland. During the day she provides consulting services to small and mid-sized businesses. But her real passion is writing emotionally charged stories of flawed people who find redemption through love and acceptance. She now lives with her husband in a beautiful town in northern Arizona.

I love to hear from my readers.

Send me an email: shirleen@shirleendavies.com
Visit my Website: https://www.shirleendavies.com/
Sign up to be notified of New Releases:
https://www.shirleendavies.com/contact/
Follow me on Amazon:
http://www.amazon.com/author/shirleendavies
Follow me on BookBub:
https://www.bookbub.com/authors/shirleen-davies

Other ways to connect with me:

Facebook Author Page:
http://www.facebook.com/shirleendaviesauthor
Pinterest: http://pinterest.com/shirleendavies

Instagram:
https://www.instagram.com/shirleendavies_author/
TikTok: shirleendavies_author
Twitter: www.twitter.com/shirleendavies

www.ingramcontent.com/pod-product-compliance
Lightning Source LLC
Chambersburg PA
CBHW061258210726
48293CB00003B/1022